playing with *Trouble*

OTHER TITLES BY JOYA RYAN

Captured Series

Break Me Slowly
Possess Me Slowly
Capture Me Slowly

Chasing Love Series

Chasing Trouble
Chasing Temptation
Chasing Desire
Chasing Mr. Wrong

Search and Seduce Series

Tell Me You Need Me
Tell Me You Crave Me
Tell Me You Want Me

Serve Series

Rules of Seduction

Reign Series

Yours Tonight
Yours Completely
Yours Forever

playing with *Trouble*

A DESIRE BAY NOVEL

JOYA RYAN

 Montlake
Romance

Text copyright © 2017 by Joya Ryan
All rights reserved.

No part of this work may be reproduced, or stored in a retrieval system, or transmitted in any form or by any means, electronic, mechanical, photocopying, recording, or otherwise, without express written permission of the publisher.

Published by Montlake Romance, Seattle

www.apub.com

Amazon, the Amazon logo, and Montlake Romance are trademarks of Amazon.com, Inc., or its affiliates.

ISBN-13: 9781503943131
ISBN-10: 1503943135

Cover design by RBA Designs

To Lauren,
Thank you for your help, kindness, and support. This
book wouldn't be what it is without you. Thank you.

Chapter One

Laura Baughman took a deep breath, smelling the sea air and the coming rain. What the hell was she doing? Oh, right, she was taking her life back. Which was why she was standing in front of her father's home-and-garden shop in the small town she'd grown up in and hadn't been back to in ten years.

A raindrop hit her nose, and she could almost hear the splat of the water lash her skin. She gasped, because it was a shock. She hadn't seen a lot of rain in the past ten years in California. Hell, being desert-bound for a decade, she'd almost forgotten what water looked like.

"Are you okay?" her friend Hannah's voice boomed through her cell phone.

"Yes, I'm fine," Laura said and wiped her nose. "Just . . . I think it's starting to rain."

"Yeah, that'll happen. It's fricking Oregon."

Laura balanced the phone between her shoulder and ear and continued to stare down her childhood. This was the shop her father and mother had started before she was even born. The shop that was supposed to be a part of her future . . . before she'd run away.

"Yes, I'm aware it rains in Oregon," Laura said defensively. It had been a long time, but she could still remember how a storm sounded when the clouds rolled above the ocean waves and surrounded the cute coastal town with a rumble of thunder. It had always calmed her. Not scared her. Because her mother loved the rain. *Had* loved it.

"Not much changes around here," Laura said, squinting to look several blocks down Main Street. The same bright-colored shops still lined the cobblestone sidewalk, and the yellow lamps in front of every store glowed softly. Her father's shop—its own structure with an acre surrounding it—was at the end of the street. Now wasn't the time to walk into town and literally down memory lane, though. She had to find her dad, who should be here—yet there was no sign of life.

"A lot more has changed than you know," Hannah said. Laura could hear people talking in the background and glasses clinking. "You coming by my bar later? Say hi to your best friend properly?"

"Of course," Laura said. She and Hannah had grown up together and stayed in touch. She really was her best friend and, honestly, the only person she'd confided in about the past and the struggle that came with it.

So much had happened in the past, and Laura was starting a mental graveyard in her mind where all her hopes had gone to die. Yep, she *had* had a lot of things, and then she'd lost them.

Laura tugged on her ring finger. Her left ring finger. The finger that had had a ring on it but was now bare. Even though it'd been a year since she'd filed for divorce, there was six months of fighting beforehand. It had taken only a few weeks for the ink to dry before she packed her few possessions in her car. And still she tugged that same finger when nervous. But she'd said good-bye to her ex-husband a long time ago. In her heart and in her life. It had been a brutal year, but she was finally healing. Over him. Over the mess that he'd made of her life. Ten years of being emotionally beaten down. Being told, convinced, that she was nothing more than what he allowed her to be. Nothing was hers. Not the money, not the career, nothing. It was all his and he'd taken it, and she was happy to be rid of him. Because she still had her spine and her ambition. And she'd lost herself there for a while, but she was ready to take back her life for herself. And claiming her family shop was the first step.

Another drop of rain hit her nose, and she shifted in her four-inch pumps. The store parking lot was riddled with chunky old asphalt, and she struggled to find a flat surface.

"Lot of cute guys in here tonight," Hannah said.

"The man I'm interested in is Waylon Wells."

"Ew, the old guy?"

"He still does concrete around here, right?" Laura asked. Her father had hired him twenty years ago to pour the parking lot in the first place.

"Ah, yeah," Hannah confirmed.

"Great." Because Laura wasn't interested in dating, or men—she was interested in getting this home-and-garden shop looking fresh and in top shape.

Hopefully without making a mess of things first. Because that was something she'd been known for. Laura Baughman: the girl who makes messes and wrong decisions. Like her ex, for example. She was the one who'd fallen for him. But that was her curse. Her mother used to tell her all the time, "Laura Baughman, you're better suited to pick a man from a hat than from your intuition." And that was fair. Considering Laura had always picked the *wrong* man. Always. But that was going to change, since not only was she back in town to pick up the pieces of a life she'd left behind, it was her final shot to make something of herself. For herself. And that meant no men. And absolutely no dating.

Yep. Zero.

Just the thought made her brain—and other parts—throb in protest, but she had to stay strong. She'd been celibate this past year going through a messy divorce; what was another year?

She shuddered at the thought. Granted, her ex, Graham, hadn't been stellar in the bedroom. Once upon a time, she was a naive nineteen-year-old and he was the older, wiser guy who'd blown through town with swagger and mystery. But she wasn't a coed or a virgin anymore. She'd given both those things to Graham, and now, with one sexual partner and a decade of disappointing nights under her belt, she could surely forgo sex and intimacy, since it wasn't like she'd been rolling in either beforehand.

"So . . . you really okay?" Hannah asked, seeming to pick up something in Laura's silence. And the truth was, no, not really. Staring at the shop with its white shutters and empty flower bed out front made her miss her mother even more. It was ten years ago this week that she'd passed away. Ten years ago that Laura had had the choice to stay and help her father with the shop, to grieve, be a good daughter, and step up. Ten years ago that she'd chosen to run from her mother's death—the pain—and follow the wrong guy right out of town and never look back. Ten years ago she'd made a lot of wrong choices. But she had been a nineteen-year-old in pain. Wasn't an excuse, but it was something she had to make right.

"I'm good," she lied. "Just need to find my dad." Her father had been kind to her. Keeping in touch, with limited phone calls from time to time. Laura had been isolated in her marriage, and the memories of her mother were too tough, so she hadn't come back to town before this. Everything had changed after her mother died. She was the warm, stable glue that kept their little unit of three together. When she passed, her father's quirks came out with a vengeance, just like Laura's flighty need to always chase something far away. They'd both lost their rock and had been free-falling ever since.

And she was sorry.

So damn sorry she couldn't look at herself in the mirror anymore. But she'd fix everything. She'd try. She'd help. And she'd make it right with her father, the shop, and her mother's memory.

"Are you back for good, then?" Hannah asked. It was the same question she'd asked several times since Laura told her she was coming home.

"Yes. That's my plan," Laura confirmed.

"Well, then you'll need something—or someone—to take out your pent-up aggression on," Hannah said. "I have a couple gentlemen at my bar right now who would be happy to show you a good time." Hannah's voice sounded a bit more distanced as she said, "Here's her picture. Yeah, she's hot, huh?"

Great. So Hannah was showing Laura's picture on her cell phone to random guys she was waiting on at the bar.

"I told you I'm not dating," Laura said.

"Dating? I'm just trying to get you laid. You're welcome."

Laura laughed. Yeah, Hannah was not only her best friend but a great wingwoman. Too bad she didn't need a wingwoman.

"Get your mind out of the gutter," she said to Hannah. Speaking of gutter, the little shop still looked the same. Only it wasn't so little anymore. The cute storefront that had once housed her mother's flowers was still adorable, but from the outside it looked more like an office than a flower shop. Odd since it was a floral shop, no matter how home-and-garden her father had tried to brand it. Her father had told her some renovations had gone on over the years and business was booming, but these weren't small renovations. She was staring down a full-blown warehouse with storefront curb appeal. Apparently Laura hadn't realized just how much business had boomed.

That's what ten years away will get you.

The large, white building with blue trim was still adorable. It was also now massive.

Last time she'd seen the place, it had been a small floral shop with a few plants and gardening supplies for sale. While the charming storefront remained, the entire place had been built up and out. The little shop was dark, but the massive warehouse that sat behind it looked well lit. It had once been her mother's dream, and now it was her own future.

BAUGHMAN HOME GOODS

A large, proud sign in the same blue and white hung in the center of the building. Might as well have been a giant middle finger to her. Because she wasn't sure how to tackle this place. It was her father's business, but when her mother had died the summer she'd graduated high school, he'd told Laura the store was hers if ever she wanted it. A place to call home. Problem was, when her mother had passed, Laura had run. Far and fast from home. Because it felt empty without the woman she'd looked up to. Her father had been devastated, too, but judging by the looks of it, the past ten years had been good to him and the business. And Laura could use a bit of home now. She had her degree in design and marketing, but she hadn't done much else over the past ten years outside of being Mrs. Graham Lincoln and slowly watching her self-esteem wither away. Which was why she was determined to not only put down roots she could be proud of, but be the woman her mother could be proud of. And it was time Laura took her life and planted some roots and succeeded.

Granted, that might be tricky, since she'd thought she'd get to run the floral shop she'd remembered. Not a gigantic home-and-garden supply store. Doubts were creeping in. The doubts that had been hammered into her head by her ex and that she was working hard at swatting away.

"Doubts you can't afford," she said, shifting again in her designer heels—one of the few things she'd gotten to keep in the divorce. Turned out, Graham had a better lawyer than she did, and Laura had escaped with her car, a couple of suitcases, and her fillings.

"Ah, crap, you're talking to yourself again. Are you sure you're okay?" Hannah asked.

"Yes," Laura said on a breath. She used to give herself pep talks, and that wasn't weird at all. Right?

Deep breath.

It was over.

Time for a fresh start.

This floral shop was hers, and staring down the building where her father had once cut dahlias for her mother, Laura knew she could make this work. This was her home. And once, a long time ago, she had been happy here. But that had vanished along with her mother. At least, she thought it had. Standing there, Laura felt closer to an answer, to her mother's spirit, than she had in a long time. And damn it, she was going to chase that.

"I've got to go. I'll see you tonight," she said to Hannah and clicked off her cell.

She headed for the front door of the shop and glanced around . . . He should be here. He'd said he'd meet her.

"Dad?" she called out as she reached the front entrance. "Daddy?" she tried again, peeking into the window and seeing no one inside. With the sky getting grayer and no sign of anyone, she was getting worried he wasn't there yet.

"Caught up in his crazy," Laura mumbled. As if her father had somehow heard her, a crash of thunder boomed.

"You've got to be kidding me," she said as another drop of freezing water splashed on her forehead.

She hustled toward the entrance and pulled open the floral shop door, only to be greeted with a nearly dislocated shoulder, because the damn thing was locked.

"Hello?" she yelled and tapped on the window next to the door. She peered inside the other window to find a darkened room with a small seating area and a few clear-doored refrigerators. Refrigerators that should have had flowers in them, but didn't.

So the flower shop was closed? On a weekday? Not a smart business move, considering the revenue the store would miss out on. That would be the first of many things she'd change around here. She might not have a lot going for her, like a home or a job or a boyfriend—not that she was looking, because that would go against her no-dating rule—but Laura was a damn fine marketing consultant. She may have struggled in her marriage, but what started as odd jobs in freelance marketing was slowly building into a career.

The warehouse was around back. It was a weekday during business hours—surely someone would be there. Maybe someone like her dad. Scatterbrained old man with a heart of gold. But because of all this, she'd have to walk around the entire building to see if the loading area was open.

Only in Oregon could the rain turn from a mild inconvenience to a damn Amazonian, end-of-the-world downpour in seconds. She trudged back into the rain, which was coming down harder. She tried not to cry when her Jimmy Choo got caught in a pothole.

"Shit!"

She tugged, but the damn thing was stuck.

Deciding she'd have to ratchet it free, she stepped out of her shoe, the coarse asphalt abrading the underside of her foot as she reached into the puddle and tried to jimmy Jimmy free from the mean pothole that was chewing up her favorite pair of stilettos.

"Come on . . . give it up, you rat bastard!" With a big yank, she launched backward, the heel snapping off, and Laura landed on her ass on the wet ground.

She looked at her shoe, which now was considered a flat. Stupid pothole.

With one shoe on and the other broken in her hand, she had nothing left to do but finish her trek around the building, where—thank the Lord—the back was open. Massive roll-up doors were open and the smell of diesel, dust, and dirt radiated from the warehouse. Machinery used to move mountains of gravel, sawdust, and lumber, it looked like. Because there were mountains of all three in there.

Holy crap, when had her dad gotten into the supply part of the home-and-garden business? This looked to be a large operation, not just a small floral shop anymore. He'd mentioned things—like that he had hired more people and business was growing—but Walt Baughman had never been one for specifics.

She stumbled in, calling out for signs of life.

She didn't know a lot about the heavy machinery side of this gig, but she knew enough to recognize a lifter-mcbob and a plow-thingy.

When she knocked her knee on a yellow machine complete with jaws, she winced, bent over, and rubbed her kneecap, a welt puffing up instantly and stinging like hell.

"This doesn't look good," Laura said to herself.

That was the exact opposite of what Jake thought, staring down the most perfect ass he'd ever seen.

The ass in question, and its owner, were soaked, kind of muddy, and in his warehouse. Talk about a great way to end the day. He'd always been an ass man. And judging by the outstanding view, including a long set of legs covered in slick rain and a fitted black skirt, he'd give this one a solid eleven out of ten.

It had been a long day up until then—he tilted his head to the side to get a better view—but it was shaping up real quick.

Jake would like to think he didn't have a type. But he did. And it was tall, blonde, and—as of just recently—wet. Still, he had to find his manners and help this clearly lost woman.

"You all right, ma'am?" he asked.

She stood, obviously shocked by his presence. "Ma'am?"

Sure, he was a man who appreciated a fine woman, but he wasn't an animal. He'd been raised by a single mother and also had a younger sister. Respect was a big deal. Granted, the mystery woman who still wasn't facing him didn't seem to like the word *ma'am*.

"I'm not a ma'am. I'm a miss," she protested. Her voice was mildly familiar.

She turned and—

"Ho-lee shit," he muttered, staring down the one girl he hadn't thought he'd ever see again. Scratch that, she wasn't a girl. She may have looked it last time she was in town. But Laura Baughman was a full-blown woman and had grown into her curves nicely. So nicely, in fact, he'd have to rethink his stance on being an ass man after all. He'd also rethink his type, because truth be told, his type was Laura Baughman. Had been since high school. But Laura Baughman had a notorious type as well, and Jake wasn't it. At least, back then.

"A poet with words," she said deadpan, accompanied with a rolling of her eyes. Christ, he hadn't meant to curse. But those eyes—rolling or not—hadn't changed much. Brown irises and thick lashes were vibrant against a perfectly tan complexion. That kind of tan wasn't seen in these parts. It reminded Jake that Laura, with her ever-apparent attitude, had spent the last decade somewhere in the sunshine. Sure, he'd heard the rumors and picked up a few details from Walt over the years. She'd run off right after high school, gotten married, and lived some grand life in some big city. He'd also heard that she wasn't married anymore . . .

"Forgive my use of *ma'am*, ma'am," he said. And nope, she definitely didn't like that. Maybe she'd lost her sense of humor? Once upon a time they had joked together and she'd laughed a lot. She was always kind. A bright sun all on her own, walking down those old school hallways. But judging from the way she barely glanced at him, only to go back to examining her knee, she didn't seem to recognize him. At all. Which meant he could work a different angle.

"You should work on broadening your vocabulary before asking for forgiveness. *Ma'am* makes me seem old and bitter, which I'm not."

"Clearly," he said. Wow, either she'd changed or she was in a bad mood. Either way, it was time to take that different approach. Because they weren't teenagers anymore, and he wasn't some lovesick puppy dreaming of the day Laura Baughman would notice him. Nope. Between the six inches of height and a hundred pounds of muscles his late growth spurt had given him roughly nine years ago, he wasn't a wimpy, shy guy anymore. And he more than knew how to talk to a lady . . .

"If you want me to sweet-talk you, all you have to do is ask." He winked at her.

That got her to face him fully. With that pretty mouth wide-open and likely ready to hand him his ass, she instead went mute, and a bright pink flush stained her cheeks.

"I, ah . . . ," she stuttered, those brown eyes going a little wide as she looked him over. Her gaze paused longer on his mouth, then his chest, then his . . . belt? Looked like Miss Baughman was checking him out. Something that had never happened back in high school. Sure, she'd been the prom queen and a knockout then, just like now, but she'd always been nice to him. Didn't mean he'd ever had a shot with her, because she was way, way out of his league.

She ran her palm over her hair as if trying to straighten it. It was golden and long and hung way past her shoulders in wet waves, which were currently dripping water from the tips of the tendrils to the cement floor. Poor woman looked drenched, disheveled, and sexy as hell.

Any minute she'd smile and realize who he was and that he was just messing with her by his earlier comment.

She shook her head, as if trying to get rid of whatever thoughts she'd been having, and returned to scowling in his direction.

Wait . . . scowling?

"I'm looking for my father, Walt Baughman. Not for you or your pickup lines."

Funny how she said, "my father, Walt Baughman," as if Jake didn't know who she was. Which meant . . .

"Do you know who I am?" he asked and gestured to his name tag with his eyes. Sure, they hadn't been BFFs in high school, but they'd hung out some. But she couldn't be this out of the loop, right? Considering her father was basically retired and Jake was running the show. Had been for the past five years now. He was even set to buy the place from Walt as soon as he was ready. Because Jake had put a decade of blood, sweat, and tears into the place, and it was like his home. His career. His purpose.

"Oh!" Laura smiled awkwardly. "Of course, Jake." She read his name tag. "You're the stock boy—man"—she caught herself—"the one my father has spoken so highly of in the past."

Jake frowned. Stock boy? Okay, he didn't look like the band geek he'd once been. Sure, his hair was longer, and he could grow a beard now, and had ditched the braces. Side note: he could still play a wicked clarinet solo. But he couldn't be *that* different.

"I'm happy to hear your father thinks highly of me, considering we built the place up together. But I'm curious what *you* think of me. Presently."

She frowned. "I, ah . . . I don't think I understand. If you want honesty, then I should tell you that your pickup line could use some work. And I'm not interested in dating Baughman employees, so . . ."

"I see your ego is still right on point," he said with a grin and hooked one thumb in his belt, which she stared at. Oh yeah, ego or not, Miss Baughman was checking out a Baughman employee.

"Says the guy who's flexing his pecs," she replied.

"So you noticed my pecs?" He flexed again, making them dance, and that pink flush in her cheeks deepened. Man, sparring with her was fun.

"Noticed or not, you clearly can't take the hint that I'm not interested in a stock boy."

"Well, *clearly* you've been misinformed, because the word you're looking for is *foreman*. Maybe if I got out my marching band uniform that'd help jog your memory and your manners?"

Her beautiful eyes went wide. She looked at his name tag again, then at his face. Name tag. Face.

"Jake . . . as in Jacob Lock?"

He smiled, because those eyes ran the entire length of his body again. Up and down and back up and back down.

"You're . . . hot—huge! I meant, huge." She clamped her hand over her mouth, but it was too late. Prom queen thought he was hot. And the nerd in him wanted to jump for joy. "I had no idea you were that Jake. I thought you were just some lug telling me my dad's business and—"

"Hitting on you?"

She nodded and laughed. "Yeah. But I was wrong because you never had a girlfriend—I mean . . . that's not what I meant. I meant you're not the type to hit on someone."

"In my defense, my line was pretty good, and I was just responding to your attitude."

That made her take an extra breath. "You think I have attitude?"

"Oh, I know you do," he said with a smile. And like it or not, Jake was both irritated and turned on. Because he did know how to treat a woman, and that was something he wanted to show prom queen over there real bad. Because she was the misinformed one if she thought he was anything like he'd been when he was a scrawny teenager.

"I didn't mean to be snarky. I just got caught in the rain, and you are the first person I've seen around here. And you're so . . ." She scanned him again. "Different."

Different.

Jake wanted to take that as a good thing, but deep down, he knew he was still the nerd talking to the popular girl, and a flare in him wanted to take that word, *different*, and replace it with another. Like, *strong, capable, hot*. Which she had said already. No takesees-backsees. Wow, even his mind was thinking like a damn teenager again.

And Laura Baughman was difficult. She wasn't a brat, exactly. She was a wild card. Went after what she wanted. He knew this because her ambition had led her straight out of town right after graduation.

"You look exactly the same," he said. And that was a lie. She looked better. So much better it wasn't fair to other humans.

"You don't at all," she said. "The you-now could eat the you-in-high-school for a snack."

"Now look who's the poet with words," Jake said.

"I just mean, it's remarkable! You grew . . . in lots of ways." She nibbled her bottom lip, and if she didn't stop that, something else was going to grow in his jeans. Looked like any hope he had of her not affecting him was gone. Because she did then, and she did now.

"Still the same me, not that I was so bad before."

"Of course not," she said. "You were great. And now you work for my dad."

"With." Jake worked *with* him. But she didn't look impressed. And she might not have meant to say that he was the stock boy earlier, but her polished facade was enough to show that she was not his type. Just like she wasn't his type back then. A decade may have passed, but they were still in different leagues. Didn't stop him from crushing hard on her, but it would stop him from repeating that giant road to nowhere again.

But damn, she was gorgeous. She wore a tight, white button-up tucked into that skirt, and he was starting to have fantasies about rucking the hem up to her hips and seeing what lay beneath. Thanks to the water, it was possible to see right through her top for a prime view of the lacy demi cups beneath. A full C, it looked like.

God bless the rain.

"So catching up is fun, but I really do need to find my dad," she said. "Do you know where he is?" With her cell phone in one hand and a busted shoe in the other, she tapped a couple of keys a few times. "He's not returning my texts."

"That's because Walt Baughman doesn't text. In fact, he doesn't usually carry his cell, either." Not that Jake had seen. Granted, Walt didn't come around a whole lot. He was more of a silent owner who popped in now and again instead of a steady worker.

She frowned at him. "I got him a phone last Christmas."

He shrugged. "Doesn't mean he uses it."

With an exasperated breath, she continued tapping on her phone.

"There's my girl!" Walt's voice boomed from behind Jake as the man walked in. His silver hair was combed back and wet from the rain, and his usual Hawaiian shirt was soaked, as were his Birkenstocks. The man always looked like he'd just walked out of a Jimmy Buffett concert, no matter the weather. He loved that man like his own father and respected him even more. He gave Jake a quick pat on the back then headed toward his daughter.

"Hi, Daddy!" She hugged him, and Jake wondered if that's what having a dad felt like. He wouldn't know, since his had taken off when he was young. But Walt was a good man and Laura was lucky to have him.

"See you've gotten reacquainted with the Oregon weather," Walt said, looking her over.

"Yeah, it'll take some getting used to. Maybe we can expand the overhang in front of the shop. I got drenched waiting out there."

"Great idea!" Walt said.

Whoa, great idea? Woman wasn't here fifteen minutes and she was already talking about major work to the outside storefront. Which cost money. Something neither Baughman paid too close attention to, since Jake had basically taken over the shop and all the details.

"Ah . . . we can talk about that," Jake said, trying not to interject but wanting to make sure he was on the same page.

Laura frowned at him. Okay, maybe he was a page off . . .

"I would love to talk about a lot of ideas I have, Dad," Laura said, clearly not interested in chatting with Jake about this. Which irked him, since he'd been here for a decade and she hadn't. But Laura always had had a knack for coming and going whenever she liked. They'd been on the student council together and she would show up randomly, turn everything he'd planned out upside down, then leave before the votes were counted. Yeah, he was well aware that Laura Baughman had ideas, and she had no problem fighting for them, no matter the time, place, or person in her way.

"Well, like I told you, sugarplum, the flower shop is all yours," Walt said.

"What's that now?" Jake said, shock going through him. When he'd started working for Walt ten years ago, Baughman Home Goods had been a small flower shop at best. But they'd built it up into a major home supplier of goods and products.

"The flower shop is mine," Laura said, like he was an idiot with a hearing problem.

"I get that, but the warehouse—"

"Is yours," Walt said, giving Jake a nod. "Jake here is responsible for all the store's success."

Laura looked between her father and him, and Jake couldn't quite read the expression on her face. But he'd bet his salary she wasn't happy.

"I don't know about all this gravel and wood." She waved her hand. "So you can go about your business with that. I'm just excited to revive the flower shop and really make it something special. Like Mom had."

"Mmm-hmm, of course, sugarplum. Whatever you want," Walt said. But the man was half paying attention now because he was tapping on—Jesus Christ—a cell phone?

"Can we back up here for a second?" Jake said. Because *whatever you want* was a dangerous phrase to use. "The warehouse doesn't sell flowers. Hasn't in years."

"Well, that's going to change," Laura said.

Jake looked to Walt for some backup and found the old man still texting.

"If you want to sell flowers, that's fine. But the warehouse and flower shop need to stay disconnected. No crossing funds, profits, or anything."

"This is about money," she said.

Well, yeah. Because the warehouse made it, and the shop didn't. So as long as that was understood up front, everything would be fine.

"I need start-up capital, and the warehouse and the shop are connected," Laura said.

"I don't sell flowers," Jake said with finality.

"And I don't work with the rocks and wood," she said.

"But you want to fix the overhang and have ideas," he started. "Which, let me guess, you'll need money for?"

"Maintenance costs are part of running a lucrative business."

Yep, this was snowballing fast, and Walt was—Jesus—was he playing Candy Crush now?

"Walt?" He got his mentor's attention.

"Yes, son?" he said.

Deep down Jake loved it when Walt called him that. But judging by the look on Laura's face, she didn't.

"Can you give some guidance here? While Laura is staying for . . . ?"

"Indefinitely," she said, but Jake had a feeling that wasn't going to happen. But one thing at a time.

"If she's running the flower shop"—with no flowers, he might add—"and the warehouse is still in business and separate, that is presenting a problem."

"Mmm," Walt said and scratched his chin. "I see your point, son." With a deep breath, he clapped his hands together and smiled. "Well, son, you run the warehouse and Laura will run the shop."

"But Daddy, they are one business. Should be run as one."

Are not! Jake wanted to spit out, but he didn't want to come off like an arguing child. He'd worked hard to build the warehouse. He made a profit from it. Laura had just showed up with a grand plan and zero funding.

"Mmm," Walt said again. "I see your point, sugarplum."

Oh, for Christ's sake. Jake was going to lose his mind.

"Well, then I guess you two will have to work it out. I'm basically retired, you know that," he said happily to Jake. And yes, Jake did know that. But officially and unofficially were different, because Walt was the owner. Not Jake. So he needed some kind of support here on how to take this little endeavor of Laura's forward—and how to survive it.

"Daddy, don't you think just one person should be in charge of it all?" Laura suggested.

"Yes, I think you're right," Walt said, and Jake's right eye began to twitch. "Jake, you run the warehouse, and Laura, you start working on flowers in the shop. After thirty days, whoever has done the best job will take over all of it. Time to make my retirement official, after all."

"What?" Jake and Laura said in unison. They only thing they seemed to agree on was that this was crazy.

"Um, Daddy, seeing as how I'm your daughter, I should have access to the business. And the flower shop will need some TLC."

Jake huffed—this was her subtle way of saying she needed money "from the business." In other words, from his warehouse.

"Of course, sugarplum. Just talk to Jake. I'm sure he's happy to work with you."

That made Jake smile and cross his arms. Finally, something he could get behind.

Laura opened her mouth—obviously to argue—but Walt got a ping on his phone and smiled.

"My lady friend just texted, looks like dinner is ready early."

Laura frowned. "Lady friend? Is she coming to the house tonight?"

"No, I'm staying with her. Have been awhile now. You can have my old place," Walt said casually. But Laura looked like she'd just been struck with a sack of sawdust.

"Dad, when did this happen? Are you two serious? Are you telling me you're living with this woman?"

"Roberta," he said. "And yes. Gotta run, sugarplum. Jake will take you to your new home. And so happy to have you back!"

It was clear where Laura got her spark from, but Walt had his quirks for sure. Because the man all but ran out, leaving Jake standing in the middle of a shit storm, which had nothing to do with the actual storm churning outside.

"What the hell just happened?" Laura said, looking at Jake, then watching her father get into his car and honk as he drove his old '83 El Camino away.

"Looks like we're working together," Jake said.

"No, he said I had to *ask* you? The floor man. Which is not happening. This shop is important to me. It was my mother's and special, and I'm here to restore it."

"It's *fore*man, and yeah, you do have to ask me when it comes to using the warehouse in any way." Which included money. "Since I know the accounts and the business plan and I run this place, that's not such a crazy request."

But Laura shook her head like she'd just been hit in the face. Like this was something devastating in her world. Was she really so stuck-up she refused to ask "the help" for . . . well . . . help?

After a long moment, she mumbled something that sounded like, "I can do this," and then faced Jake.

"Don't mistake this crazy scheme my father has set up as me reporting to you, or me somehow putting my life in your hands. I'm doing this on my own. And I'm not going to tolerate you telling me what to do."

Those words came out harsh, like they'd been broken from deep in her chest, but Jake couldn't think about why right now. Whatever she'd done the past ten years wasn't his business. Baughman Home Goods was his business, though. And he'd make sure it stayed in good shape and in the black.

"And stop with the muscles," she said, looking at his chest again. "Get a baggier shirt, for God's sake, I can see everything."

He smiled. "So does this mean you don't want to join the company softball team?"

She rolled her eyes.

The woman might irritate him, but she had his heart racing in a way he hadn't felt in a long time.

A challenge.

And she wasn't as immune to his charms as she'd like to pass off, because she was back to staring down at his belt. So he flashed her a smile and flexed for good measure.

"If you think I won't go after what I want, you're mistaken. Because I will. And this flower shop is mine. And the entire business will be, too, since it *is* connected. So I hope you enjoy working under a Baughman."

Oh, he could get on board with doing a lot more than working under her.

"You know, I do enjoy my job very much. Actually"—he leaned in a little—"rumor is, I get to work here as long as I want for the rest of my life."

Oh, she did not like that statement, because her scowl hardened and her pretty face looked ready to crack with fury. But she'd heard Walt same as he had. This was up to them. Thirty days to show how each ran a business. Walt would retire, and good thing for Jake. He'd already been doing a pretty good job running the business so far. He wasn't interested in destroying Laura's dreams. In fact, he would continue to think of the warehouse and shop as separate.

"You know what they say about rumors?" she said in a calm, vicious tone. "They make an ass out of you."

He frowned. "I think you're mixing up your sayings."

"Nope, I said it right."

A low hum worked its way up his chest. He'd forgotten how much fire she had. They'd never been enemies. But they were never overly close. He wasn't a band geek pining for her attention anymore. He was in charge of the Baughman legacy, the warehouse, and the business funds. Being friends with her had been nice, but fighting with her was kind of fun—a new development that, as of now, got him hot. Laura Baughman was a challenge *and* a turn-on. One look at her told him she'd forfeit her flower shop endeavor the moment one of her manicured nails broke. Another part of him wanted to believe in her. But he didn't know Laura like he had ten years ago. Who knew what she was willing to do and where she was willing to run? Because while he didn't know the details, she'd run away from home once, only to run right back.

He'd never expected Laura to ever come home, and honestly, Jake had never thought she'd really claim any part of the business if she did. And she already had ideas. Something he'd get to the bottom of, but first he had to make her aware of this situation.

"I understand you're excited about the flower shop. But the warehouse is what makes the money. The shop is mostly an office and—"

"And I'm going to change that. There's no flowers in there. It looks more like an office."

"Well, because it is."

"No, it's going to house and sell flowers."

"So you're talking about start-up capital, and that is something we need to discuss, because the profit comes from the warehouse."

"This is my family's business, and that means that it's part of whatever it is you've been doing the past few years."

"Ten," he said, getting aggravated. "*Ten* years. Same number of years you've been gone, having no idea what's going on. Now you're here, ready to claim a business when it looks like you just lost a fight with a mud puddle," he said.

"It was a pothole, and it was particularly aggressive, I assure you. In fact"—she waved her hand, which was still gripping a busted shoe, in his direction—"that's something that should be fixed."

He laughed. The woman wasn't even here for a full twenty minutes and she was dishing out orders? Typical. She was a different breed from him. He'd known that back in high school. But it seemed Laura was coming in feisty, and Jake's patience was being tried. Because the business, Walt, his family, and this town meant everything to him. That couldn't be risked or messed with. Not even by a Baughman herself.

Walt worked with his hands. He had taken Jake in when he was eighteen and given him a job. His own dad had split when he was young, and he was the oldest. He had his mother and sister to take care of. And Walt had given him the opportunity to be the man his family could depend on.

Which was why preserving what he and Walt had built, his legacy, was so important to him. Jake wanted to buy the business so it could be run correctly and make Walt proud even after retirement. Unfortunately, nearly all of the equity he'd put into the company was sweat. And it was still Walt's. And Walt wasn't very helpful in settling disputes.

"You can't start barking orders when I'm not even sure you'll last a week here," Jake said.

Her gaze shifted, like his words cut her somehow. She opened her mouth to yell, maybe defend herself, then snapped it shut. She thrust her chin in the air and said, "This is my home and my hometown, and I'm here for the long haul. The past doesn't matter, and it's none of your business anyway. I'm here now. Claiming the flower shop. And"— she clasped her hands together and glanced around—"there's a lot that needs to be done around here."

Jake agreed. The warehouse was constantly busy, and he was always either hauling bark or visiting construction sites to drop off lumber.

Baughman Home Goods' biggest moneymaker was what went on behind the poor excuse for a gardening shop out front. They were the key supplier of lumber and rock in the area. No one came in for flowers; they came in for supplies. Hell, they didn't even stock and sell flowers anymore. This turn in the business was what had kept Walt from going under years back. And Jake would make sure it stayed that way.

"I want a key to the floral shop door," Laura said.

He chuckled. "Honestly, Laura, all kidding aside. How long do you think you'll last here? Your quote in the yearbook was 'Never stay still and always chase the bigger and better.'"

She looked at him dead in the eye. "Well, that was then. I'm home now. And I'll be home long enough to outlast you and make these thirty days skyrocket in profit and prove I can run this place."

Oh, that got his blood heating another degree. He pushed off the forklift he'd been leaning against and invaded her personal space. "Don't bet on that. I have more stamina than you can imagine."

Her lips parted and her shaky inhale was the only indication that he was getting to her. Which was exactly what he needed to be doing. Because the air was charged with heat, aggression, and passion. He was ready to kiss her, swat her ass, make her beg and scream his name. All of it. Which was a bad idea. She was wrong for him, and the boss's daughter to boot. He was set to take over and he wouldn't go risking his reputation—especially with Walt—or the business on Laura's ideas. Besides, she had a track record for blowing in like a tornado only to run off after the damage was done. The sooner she was ready to either stay or quit, the sooner Jake could officially take over for Walt and officially get over Laura. Something he hadn't realized was a problem until just today.

At the very least, he had to make her see that this was a hard business. He also had to try to get his dick under control, because Laura Baughman was standing in front of him ripe for the picking. She was also a distraction. For God's sake, he was hard just from staring down her wet top, mile-long legs, and incredible ass.

"Come on, Laura . . . whether it's now or in a few days, the end is the same. You'll run right back to where you came from."

"You're wrong. This is my home. My business. And this is where I'm staying."

"You don't sound sure about that," he challenged.

"I am."

"Because you're so good at sticking around?" he said.

She frowned. Like he'd hurt her feelings. Which wasn't what he was going for—he just needed her gone. Already she was messing with his mind. So he slapped on a smile like she didn't affect him and watched her throat bob on a hard swallow.

Jake wasn't sure what he was doing. What he did know was that he was drawn to her. If she was going to be around for any length of time, that was going to be a problem. Call it crazy or stupid or full-on lust, but he was feeling all three for the blonde before him, and that needed to stop.

"I'm staying. And there's nothing and no one who can push me away," she said with finality. But he didn't miss her perusal of him.

Her gaze drifted to his mouth and her words were coming out a little raspier than before. Oh yeah, he affected her, too. Another reason he needed to get her high-class—perfect—ass away from him. Which would be tricky, considering she was all up in his space.

"One more thing." She took a step closer. "Don't get too comfortable, Jacob." Another step, and her voice was low and made his jeans impossibly tight. "This little stunt my father pulled with his 'Work it out, kiddos' isn't going to last forever." She trailed a finger down his chest, giving sight to the fighter in her. "My first order of business is to make this *my* business. You never know—you may want to leave all on your own."

With that, she turned on the only heel she had left and strutted that sweet ass away, deeper into the warehouse, leaving him raging pissed and desperate as hell to go another round with her—preferably in his bed.

Because there was no way he was going anywhere. The battle was set. And Jake was playing for not only his own livelihood, but Walt's legacy and the only business he'd ever had.

∽

"Deep breath . . . ," Laura told herself as she limped around the large pieces of machinery and away from the sinfully sexy Jacob Lock. He'd filled out quite a bit since she'd seen him last. He should be nothing more than an annoying obstacle. Not tall, dark, muscular, and . . . did she mention sexy?

It'd taken everything she had to feign confidence, because when she laid eyes on him, a few more puzzle pieces slid into place, and they hurt. Her father had trusted Jacob. Clearly, he was the one who had been running the business. Sure, she had a place at the flower shop and her mother's memory and wishes with that. But her father loved Jake. Trusted him. And now she more or less had to go through Jake? She'd spent the last decade being kept on a leash by her ex, and her fresh start and penance to her mother were now dictated by Jake's grace?

No.

It broke her heart thinking of that. She needed to change . . . every-thing. She couldn't go back, no matter how much she wished she could. She could only move forward, and she would. She'd keep her promise to her mother to make sure the flower shop lived on. Even though it had taken her a long time to find her way, Laura was finally home, and she felt like she just might be heading in the right direction for the first time in ten years.

She hadn't meant to be snippy with Jake, but between catching her off guard and now her father's stipulations, Jake was an obstacle. A giant, sexy, chiseled obstacle that she had to get past for the sake of her soul and her mother's memory. Because if Jake was set to run the busi-ness as a whole, the shop would be gone forever. He obviously didn't care about it; otherwise it would be open now.

She'd prove her worth. That she didn't need babysitting or to go through Jake for anything. She'd do this on her own. That was the point. But Jake was making that—and her no-dating rule—really difficult at the moment. Celibacy sucked, and it was wearing on her. Especially since Jake was right—he was not the same as he'd been high school. He looked more than capable of handling a woman's pleasure.

But she wouldn't daydream about that. There were too many other questions she had to sort through. But she knew two things: first, this was her chance to try to build a life and get closer to her mother's memory, and second, Jacob Lock was the son her father had never had.

Her father valued him. Maybe her father *wanted* to leave his legacy to Jacob? Either way, he'd given her the chance to run the shop. And she wouldn't fail. Because she still had a shot to have it all and make her mother proud.

She shook her head, warding off the pity party. She wasn't going to let the past rule her. All the awful insecurities that had been drilled into her head that she was flighty, useless . . . no. She wouldn't listen to that. She'd made a promise to herself that she would be strong. Assertive. This was her moment to be anyone she wanted to be. And she wanted to be her mother's daughter. One she could be proud of. One who didn't run away.

She also needed hope for the future since she had very little in the present other than this opportunity. And she'd cling to that. She might be in over her head—she looked up to the lifter thingy's jawlike bucket *literally* over her head—but she was smart and a hard worker. Sure, she'd been popular and the prom queen, but that—along with her spotty record of bad choices in men whom she'd had to prove herself to—was exactly why this fresh start was so important. She was determined to make the most of this chance.

Surely, she could do this. Run the office and shop and contribute. She could make Baughman Home Goods a bigger success than ever. Outshine the warehouse, even! Okay, maybe that was a bit ambitious, but she'd learn and she'd help. Granted . . . she just wanted to run a flower shop, not lumber and gravel central. But still, she could do it. And her first order of business was to revive the flower shop. She had a month to figure her life out and turn a profit before her father would intervene and make Jake her permanent boss—or her his.

Jacob was going to be a problem, though. If she were honest, she'd admit that she was attracted to him. Looked a little long at his chiseled jaw and firm, full lips. Wondered what it'd feel like to be on the receiving end of all that strength and power . . .

Good thing she wasn't being honest.

Nothing about this situation was great. But she'd manage. She had to. For once in her life, she would come through for herself. She was used to being alone, used to being underestimated, but this time? She needed a win. And she couldn't let Jacob Lock, with his persuasive mouth or rock-hard body, distract her. He was the competition.

Her mind was clouded with thoughts of their encounter. Every syllable his husky voice had uttered had made her want to choke on all her words, because what she was greeted with was more than a surprise—it was shocking.

He was six-plus feet of solid muscle. In a fitted blue T-shirt that had oil and dirt smeared on it and low-slung blue jeans that were worn to perfection in every possible way, he could easily pass as a member of the superhero squad. Not the band alum and nerd she remembered.

He was a little dirty, a lot down-home, and not big city in the slightest. A trait she kind of liked. Because the mere way he wore that brown leather belt and those scuffed-up work boots made her hormones jump for joy.

Yeah, she had been staring. She was also painfully aware that she resembled a drenched, lopsided poodle. He pulled off the damp look better than she did. The moisture from the rain made his T-shirt cling to his skin, giving her a glimpse of a perfectly chiseled chest and abs.

But all that didn't matter. He was the one person that was the exact kind of wrong. Did she want to stop pining for men she had to prove herself to? Wanted to stick to her no-dating rule? Then she needed to stay far away from Jacob Lock. Because even thinking of dating made her think of sex, so that was a bad idea, too. He obviously wasn't her biggest fan. So for now, it was wise to forget the way those icy-blue eyes made her wet body even wetter.

"Already lost? The exit is back that way." That same raspy voice belonging to her newly acquired nemesis boomed out. He accompanied his words with a hiked thumb in the direction she'd come.

"Does anyone work around here?" she snapped. Desperate to find someone that wasn't him.

"Yeah. Me. A lot. The crew took off at four."

"Why?"

"Because there was one last delivery that I could handle myself. And Carl's son had a T-ball game he needed to get to. No sense in keeping on good men and having them miss important stuff just for the sake of an hour."

She glanced down the front of him. Yes, she believed that. The man was built to handle lots of things. Heavy machinery included. And he was nice, too? Of course, he'd always been nice. He also used to wear headgear. Which was what she was trying to focus on instead of how perfectly straight and white his teeth were.

"What about the floral shop? Dad always kept it open until five. It doesn't look like it's been open all week."

He looked at her for a long moment. "It hasn't been open for a lot longer than that. We don't go in there much, unless we're doing payroll or the books. The majority of our business happens out back."

She glanced around, trying not to let her heart hurt with that tidbit of news. The floral shop was the only part of this whole operation she thought she could handle. And like Jake had said earlier, it was a glorified office. First rule in marketing was understanding what your business was selling. So like it or not, she had to understand the business as a whole. Including the warehouse.

"So bark dust and gravel?" she asked. "That's what all this is? That's the business now?"

"Home and garden supplies," he corrected.

"But the *garden* shop is closed. And flowers are part of what this place is known for."

"*Was* known for," he said. "We deal with big projects now. We have a steady cast of usual customers that keep us comfortably busy all year. Like people needing lumber for houses and sod for landscaping design. The flower shop is ambience and holds the copy machine, but that's about it."

"It should be open," she argued.

"You know how many corsages you'd have to sell to even come close to the kind of profit I get from one bark supply order?"

"Clearly *you* don't even know that comparison, since the place is closed!" she snapped. The one good memory she had was of the flower shop. It had been lovely once upon a time. It had also been booming back then. Now it was just a glorified storefront of what once was, while Jacob Lock sold manly supplies out of the warehouse in the back.

"If you want it open more, then come in and run the shop, Miss Owner."

"That's what I intend to do."

"Great," Jake said, and she could tell from his tone it was anything but great.

"Well, then." She looked around. That bounce in her step—which came from rainy-day shoe destruction instead of walking on sunshine—was starting to physically hurt, and her confidence was dissipating. She had no idea what she was expecting, or even what to do now. She had suitcases waiting and a broken shoe, and currently she was staring down the only man who had made her feel hot and bothered in a long time. He was also the man her father loved. Walt may have left her the flower shop, but he'd left everything else to Jacob. Including job security.

Wait . . . not *everything*.

"My father said I basically have the house to myself, since he's living with"—she swallowed back the horror—"his girlfriend." A topic she'd dive into later with him.

"That's right. You have his old place."

Finally, something resembling peace was on the horizon. She couldn't wait to get back to the home she'd grown up in. With the dahlia garden in back. Would it still be there? She could cut flowers and remember her mother. Remember the good moments. Maybe bring a bunch of them to the shop the way they used to and put arrangements in the cooler and start the floral shop off right.

Jacob smiled, those straight white teeth making her dizzy. Her breasts, however, were on full alert, standing to attention at the sight of his lips spreading. Where was a set of headgear when you needed it, because Jake Lock was too damn handsome for his own good and she needed a distraction from his perfect face and his stupid perfect teeth.

"I'd be happy to take you there." He grinned. The way he said that made her think he knew a secret she didn't. "I'll lock up, bring the truck around, and you can follow."

"I know how to get to my old house."

"That's not where I'm taking you."

Before she could ask more, he turned to leave.

"Follow me and stay close."

She nodded. But she had the feeling that—irritation, frustration, and expectations aside—being near Jacob Lock was a bad idea, especially when her mind was churning out thoughts of just how much of her skin those big hands of his could cover.

This was going to be more stressful than she'd realized.

Chapter Two

"It's beautiful," Laura said, looking at the large house on the outskirts of town. Her father must have built a new house! It was an A-line cottage style with massive windows and surrounded by trees. It was a far cry from the small house Laura had grown up in. Maybe he'd planted a garden out back?

"Thanks," Jacob said, shutting his truck door and grabbing Laura's suitcases out of her trunk. The rain had let up, which was nice, since her suitcases would have gotten drenched otherwise. "Took a year to build."

"*You* built this?"

He came to stand beside her, her suitcases still in his hands. "Yep. Walt and I did a few summers back, after he sold his other house."

When Laura saw the smile and pride that lit up Jacob's face as he looked at the home, she realized that he had a very different relationship with her father than she did. Especially since she'd hadn't been around.

"He sold the house?" she asked softly.

Jacob nodded. "Yeah, the owner cleared the land and is rebuilding on it himself, I think."

"So it's gone? The house . . . the garden?" And he'd never told her. In all those phone calls, he'd never once mentioned selling her childhood home. Where her mother had had her garden. The owner had cleared the land and was rebuilding.

Jacob shrugged. "Walt wanted a fresh start, I guess. Sold it a few years ago."

Her heart beat slower and her chest tightened. Her father had sold the only tie to her childhood home, and it was gone. While the floral shop needed TLC, he'd built this house with Jacob?

But being in the presence of the house, knowing her father had used his two hands to build something with Jake, cut deeper than she wished.

And whose fault is that?

Hers.

She'd been in California chasing a man who'd degraded her, and a dream that had landed her right back in this small town.

A pang of envy hit her hard, and it felt a lot like a sharp knife to the kidney. She could never build a house, much less something like this, but she could try to rebuild the shop. And she'd stay focused on that. And at least her father had built this beautiful house, which was something. She could empathize with needing a fresh start and would never fault him for needing the same thing.

"Well, it's very nice." She walked toward the front door. She was in desperate need of a hot shower and a stiff drink. "Do you have the key?"

"I do." Again, he smiled like he'd won some victory that Laura wasn't aware of, so she continued her walk toward the house. "Where are you going?" he asked when she reached the steps to the large wraparound porch.

"Inside."

"But I didn't invite you in. That there is my house. Your place is right over there." He pointed to the left, and that's when she saw it. A few yards off to the side of the house was an old camper that had seen better days.

"You can't be serious."

"Yes, ma'am. That's your dad's, and he said earlier that it's all yours." He winked and strutted over and dropped her suitcase down in front of the camper. That envy that she'd been feeling earlier morphed into full-blown anger—and, if she were honest, total, humiliating sadness.

"He built a house with you and lived in a camper?" It wasn't a question, but it came out that way because Laura still couldn't believe it. Not that she thought she was entitled, but she had thought her father had at least had a house. Or an apartment. But a camper?

"A camper that's now all yours. Lucky lady."

Whatever expression she wore made Jacob take a step closer, that sky-blue gaze locked on her face—like he was mentally doing long division. Either that or it was a look of concern. Her money was on long division, though.

She straightened her shoulders. Letting the competition see weakness wasn't wise. And she needed to regroup, because it was clear that Jacob wanted her kept under his heel, and she wanted him to realize she was in charge of this shop endeavor. The race was on as to see who could outlast whom. She glanced at her new home. Whether it was a camper or not, she just needed some time to let this all sink in. And she needed that shower before going to meet Hannah at the bar.

"I, ah . . ." Jacob gripped the back of his neck and looked over his shoulder at his home. His *beautiful* home. The home he'd built with *her* father. He almost looked . . . sorry. As in, sorry for her. "I can take you to the grocery store later if you need. Or I have sandwich stuff if you're hungry?"

She swallowed, because she'd been right. In that moment, he felt sorry for her. Her belly growled at the offer of food, but no way would she take anything more from him. She wanted to fade away. Get a good distance between herself and those piercing eyes before they saw right through her fake confidence and she broke down in tears.

"I know where the store is and I can take care of myself, thank you." She picked up her suitcase, bumped his shoulder as she passed him, and hoisted herself into the camper.

"Suit yourself," he grumbled and strode the ten feet it took to reach his home.

So much for keeping a distance.

~

That woman wasn't just a sexy pain in the ass, she was stubborn as hell and set on making Jake's life miserable. At least the part in his jeans, because he'd been hard since he saw her bending over and now he was just getting grouchy about it.

He grabbed a beer from the fridge, popped the top, and sank his big body on his even bigger leather sofa and looked out the front windows. Though it was still gray and night was coming, it had stopped raining for now. Jake, however, couldn't stop thinking of Laura Baughman, who was now his next-door neighbor.

When she had realized that this was his house, a sadness had washed over her and he'd almost felt bad. He'd expected her to go off about her accommodations being less than adequate or give him some kind of hell about the camper, but she hadn't. She'd just stared, as if the fact that Walt had built this with him had hit a nerve.

"Not your problem," Jake reminded himself. Because she hadn't been around and he wasn't going to feel bad for the fact that he had been. So why the hell was he thinking of those big brown eyes and how they looked a little glossy after seeing the house?

Shit. Maybe she was upset. Her dad had sold her childhood home, which was clearly news to her. Maybe he should ease up on her. Maybe she was more delicate than she appeared—

His front door crashed open and there, standing in nothing but a small, tattered towel, drenched from head to toe, was Laura Baughman.

"What the hell!" she yelled.

Okay, so he'd been wrong in thinking her a delicate flower. Because what stood before him was a buck twenty of pissed-off, nearly naked, dripping-wet female. And he couldn't find a reason to be upset about that. He leaned forward, beer in hand, and rested his forearms on his bent knees.

"Sure, come on in. No need to knock or anything," he said, trying to keep his cool. But it was suddenly difficult to swallow for some reason.

"Don't give me that. What did you do to my water?" she said, stomping inside, clutching that thin towel around her chest. That hard-dick syndrome he'd had been fighting for the past hour got worse.

Full cleavage threatened to spill over the top of the scrap of fabric that barely covered her, giving him a prime view of just how long those tan legs were. And wouldn't you know, Miss Baughman must prefer itsy-bitsy bikinis in the California sun she came from, because he couldn't see a tan line anywhere.

"I didn't do anything to your water, in fact, I hooked my hose to the camper myself. You're welcome."

"Your hose?" she said with shock. "There's no hot water. I got into the shower and found that out the hard way."

"I can see that." And boy, could he. Goose bumps pricked her flawless skin, and her nipples were straining against the towel. Jake thought he might lose his goddamn mind if she stood there like that for one more second.

The woman either needed to invest in muumuus and turtlenecks or he was going to have a real problem resisting her. Which meant he needed to try extra hard to keep his distance.

Then it hit him—this setup might not have been so grand after all. His eighteen-year-old self would have given his left arm to be in the position he was in right now. Laura Baughman, nearly naked, and privacy. She also seemed to be attracted to him . . . Was he supposed to ignore that?

Yes!

Damn his stupid conscience.

So in the meantime he had to stare down the sassy vixen who both tempted and annoyed him endlessly like the piece of candy he couldn't have, and just . . . ignore her? Fat chance.

Maybe he could really push her buttons. Time to call a new play and blitz with seduction. He may not have played football in high school, but the band had had to attend games regularly. Besides, Jake had been told he looked like a linebacker, so that was close enough. He'd call the blitz play. There was a spark between them, and if she was hell-bent on sticking around, he would have to face her and all this sexual frustration daily.

Why not try to get it out of his system now, or make a move and have her shut him down and hate him? Was this brilliant or crazy? He didn't know, because he was too focused on that little towel and how *little* it really was. She seemed determined to stay . . . but he had some doubts about that. But if she did leave, better to know sooner than later. At the very least he could push some buttons and get her to want to stay away from him. Yeah, this had to be a good idea . . . not crazy. He could put the moves on and when she huffed in disgust and bolted, he could finally get some peace. Time to play a big hand and call her bluff.

Good plan.

He rose and closed the distance between them. She watched his every step as he got closer. To her credit, she didn't back away.

"You know, I'm a reasonable man." He paused to take a swig of his longneck and noticed how her eyes riveted to the action. Either Miss Baughman wanted a drink or she just liked looking at his mouth. Yep, he needed to take care of this infatuation ASAP. And since he couldn't lay her down to do it, he'd have to send her running.

So he'd piss her off.

"If you ask real nice," he said, "I'll let you use my shower."

She scoffed. "Why don't I have my own hot water?"

"Because you need a device to heat it, which you don't have."

"Obviously!" She motioned to the front of herself. "What do I need to make it hot?"

"I can make it hot for you. You just have to say the word."

She took a deep breath, and damn, he liked what that did to her breasts. Made them inch just a bit more out of the top of that towel, which was now number one on his list of things he currently hated. Time to show Miss Baughman that he wasn't the band nerd anymore. He was a man who had more than enough experience to give her exactly what she needed.

"I can't live like this," she said in a breathy voice.

"You'll need a generator to heat the water."

"What's that?"

He stalled. "You want to own a home-supply business and you don't know what a generator is?" Shit, this was worse than he thought.

"It's a home-and-garden business, which once upon a time was a flower shop. I think I can handle it. And"—she waved a finger in his face—"I *do* own it. My name is Baughman, remember?"

"Your father owns it, and I'm the one that knows about the business—and what a generator is—*remember?*"

She huffed again and Jake was one deep breath away from seeing everything he'd dreamed of when he was a teenager.

"If you just meet me halfway," he said, trying to find some common ground, literally, "I'm happy to give you what you need."

"You have no idea how much I need—"

She caught herself, and Jake wanted to know what she'd been about to say. So he pushed.

"I think I know what you need . . ." His voice was deeper than he'd meant.

"Yeah, well, what I need is something I refuse to have, so I'll just stick with the hot water."

This piqued his interest. "I hope we're talking about the same thing."

She raised a brow and crossed her arms, which did amazing things for her cleavage.

"I'm not dating anyone, Jake. So don't even try."

"Oh, I'm not trying to *date* you."

Her mouth parted, and he smiled.

"Well, I'm not having sex, either. It's a vow to myself," she said. But herself didn't look entirely on board with that statement.

"Why in the hell would you make that vow?"

"Because I need to stay focused. And the one person I was with before didn't leave me missing anything, so it's fine."

"Whoa, back up, did you say *one?*" Jake asked in shock.

Her eyes went wide, as if she'd just dished a secret she hadn't meant to. *Holy shit, the prom queen has only been with one man.*

"It doesn't matter," she said. "I'm simply telling you this so you understand where my priorities are. With the shop, not with you."

Time to get sneaky.

"Uh-huh. So you are aware of your attraction to me?" he asked.

"Of course I'm aware. I mean, look at you!"

That made him smile and her frown once again. He always had loved her mouth. Especially when it was spilling admissions about him and how much she was attracted to him.

But now he was not only aware that the gorgeous Miss Baughman had only had one sexual partner in the past ten years, but that she didn't seem to miss it. Therefore she hadn't been properly loved. Which made Jake want to rectify that situation real bad.

But she had her rules. No dating. No sex.

She seemed less firm on that last rule, though. And what constituted sex in her mind?

Perhaps it was time to find out.

Yep, he was full of good plans today, especially since his brain seemed to be in his jeans at the moment.

"Me being here and running the business is something you should get used to," she said and put a hand on her hip while the other was still busy clutching the knot of the towel around her chest.

So they were back to this. He was getting nervous, because she kept referring to the shop and the warehouse as "the business" as a whole. And that made his eye tic come back. Demanding money for her flower shop ideas was one thing. "The business" was another. Because that business—a.k.a. the warehouse—was his business.

If Miss Baughman wanted to play tough with all her talk and rules, so be it.

"Fine. Enjoy your cold shower." Keeping his eyes on her, he waited for her move. Laura Baughman was a walking, talking game of Texas Hold'em. He'd give her credit, she had a good poker face, but if he called her bluff enough, eventually she'd fold.

She stood still, dripping on his hardwood floor, and what he wouldn't do to lick those beads of water sliding down her neck and thighs. Damn, he wanted to make her drenched and dripping in a different kind of way.

She looked at her feet for a long moment, as if debating her options.

"I just need a hot shower," she finally mumbled.

"Okay." This was good! She was coming close to that common ground. Now if only he could stop thinking about making her come . . . He stood and walked toward her, not stopping until he was close enough to feel her breath. "I can help you with that," he rasped, leaning in enough to make sure she felt his body heat.

She eyed him, obviously annoyed, but there was a flash of desire in those molasses eyes, and that got his blood pumping a little faster. She might be freezing her ass off, but she felt the pull between them, too—that much was obvious.

"You're not going to be satisfied until I beg, are you?" she asked.

"Oh, I'd love it if you begged. But in a very different way than you're thinking." With his grip fastened around the long neck of his beer, he slowly ran his knuckles up her thigh, making even more goose bumps break out. "But for a shower? I'd be happy with a simple *please*."

She pressed her lips together, as if her pride willed her to remain stubborn. Time to push. Because if he didn't, he'd keep coming after her. He knew it. Laura Baughman was his kryptonite, and had been since high school. She needed to push him away and stay away, or he'd keep coming for her. Despite the consequences.

"Look at yourself," he cooed, inching just a little closer until the tips of her breasts brushed his torso. She sucked in a breath, and so did he. Because he could feel those pebbled peaks stabbing through the thin towel and the cotton of his shirt, raking against him. "Look how cold you are. You must be aching . . ." Closer still, until his mouth was right over hers. "Desperate for something . . . hot."

"I am," she breathed. When she looked at his lips, then licked her own, he was ready to pounce. Sweep her up and toss her on the couch, rip that stupid towel away and bury himself inside her until, yes, she begged. Begged him to never stop.

But he went slowly. This was a battle of wills, after all.

"Then just say the word and I can make life easier for you," he said.

She looked down, and he was pretty sure she could see firsthand the effect she had on him. She blinked a few times, a fog lifting from her brown eyes. Shock plagued her face. She glanced at his cock, which was obviously and painfully tenting his jeans, and Lord have mercy, she bit her bottom lip.

"Looks like I'm the one making things hard on you," she whispered. "And I don't need you to make anything easy on me, Jacob Lock. Because I can guarantee you there's nothing easy about me."

With that, she spun and walked out his door, that world-class ass swaying and bare feet slapping against the hardwood as she made her way out the front door, leaving him with his own hardwood problem and in need of a cold shower himself.

"Believe me, I'm well aware of that fact," he called after her.

Her response was the slamming of his front door.

Chapter Three

Laura had never needed a drink so badly in her life. That cold shower of hose water did nothing to calm her nerves after her encounter with Jacob. She was desperate for vodka and her best friend. Which were both on the other side of the bar door.

She parked around back and stared at the ocean for a moment. The town had been built along the sturdy cliffs lining the Pacific, and with the vast blue water as an endless backdrop, it was easy to feel small in a big world that was currently wrapped up in a tiny town.

Speaking of blue, Jake's eyes are incredible . . .

Shut up, brain!

Frickin' Jake.

She pinched the bridge of her nose and thanked whatever God was looking out for her that she'd mustered the courage to walk away from him earlier. Because a very big part of her had wanted to stay. The way he looked at her was hotter than any water she'd hoped for.

How had he done that? He brought out conflicting emotions. Made her feel so uncomfortable, so annoyed, so . . . *hot*. Hannah had told her about hate screwing. Apparently, people who didn't like one another still hooked up, and it was supposed to be intense and fun. Hot, even. *Hot* being a key word in Laura's world lately. Because she was either raging hot or freezing cold . . . both of which were Jacob's fault.

Yep, time for a drink.

She got out of her car and walked around to Main Street. Yachats, Oregon, on a Friday night wasn't exactly hopping. It was, however, alive. The cobblestone sidewalk was the same as she remembered, a light gray stone that always seemed a bit damp from the sea breeze. The ocean crashed in the background and was only 172 steps from the town square. She knew because she'd counted when she was eight. Nothing had changed, and it felt like home.

The salt in the air was comforting, and for a moment, she could feel her mother's voice on the wind. She was home. Now she just had to keep it that way. It took effort to thrive. And that's what she'd do.

She opened the door to Goonies, the local bar, and took two steps inside. She would have taken three, but Hannah's loud screech stopped her, and the black-haired beauty was sprinting from behind the bar and straight at her.

"Look at you!" Hannah said, hustling to Laura with spread arms. "I've missed you!"

Hannah all but crashed into her, and Laura felt so much love in the one hug.

"I've missed you, too," Laura said and hugged her friend. Even though she'd been in California the past ten years, they had stayed close over Skype and the phone. Hannah had visited a handful of times and was her best friend since birth. No distance would ever change that. Laura's father never came out to California despite Laura offering to buy his ticket. So she was grateful she had Hannah.

"So you work here now?" Laura said, looking around.

"Yep, hoping to do more than just work here one day. Maybe own," Hannah said, looking around with pride. The place was rustic and fun. Smelled like roasted peanuts and saltwater taffy and beer. Ah, a bar on the ocean. Some smells never changed.

"You didn't have to dress up for me," Hannah said, looking her over. Hannah was in a tank top and ripped jeans and a black lap apron.

Laura looked down the front of herself. Sleek black pants paired with her last and now the only pair of heels she owned—which were bright red. Gotta love getting cleaned out in a divorce. Truth was, she was happy to start fresh. She hadn't entered the marriage with much, and she'd left it just the same. She didn't want her ex or his money or any ties to him. Which was why she'd walked away. But her outfit had her second-guessing how long she'd been gone. She thought a white top was casual, Friday-night evening wear. It was back in California. But judging by the crowd, she was wrong about her outfit. Very, very, wrong.

"I, ah . . ." Laura felt the sudden sense that while a lot hadn't changed around Yachats—including the pool table off to the left, the massive open space near the corner stage where local bands came in to play, and even the LIFE'S A BEACH sign made of green paint and distressed wood hanging in the same place—she had, and it was her old small-town self she was trying to re-find.

"You look great," Hannah said and clasped her hand. "Come have a drink." She walked behind the bar and started refilling the cups of the patrons while Laura took a minute to look around. Wood floors that creaked with every step like a song. Ocean themes, like antique harpooning gear and shark teeth, scattered on the walls. She'd missed this place. Casual and simple and home.

But the longer she stood there, the more she felt out of place. Odd since it was home and yet felt so distant. Maybe she was more lost in her life than she'd thought.

Despite the country music blaring from the jukebox, she heard mumbles of her last name being thrown around. People around here apparently remembered who she was—or rather, whose daughter she was. But it was a small town. People usually *knew of* everyone at the very least.

Clearing her throat and deciding that she'd made it this far, she moved to get that drink. She walked to the bar counter, keeping her eyes forward as a woman with teased bangs and a leopard-print tank top stared her down.

She flashed a smile, and leopard woman smiled back. Brightly.

"Hi there, honey," the woman said. She closed the few steps between them with intent strides, make her triple Ds shake and sway as she yanked Laura in for a hug.

Okay, so that was a fail in the politeness department, and Laura had no idea what to do. She couldn't do much of anything other than inhale the unmistakable scents of spandex and White Diamonds perfume. The overly nice and apparently personal-space-unaware stranger was concerning, because the hug was lasting way longer than social norms would dictate.

"You are just gorgeous!" the woman said, clasping Laura's shoulders and shoving her back to look her over. Laura felt like a rag doll next to the voluptuous woman intent on pawing at her. "My God, you look nothing like your father. So you must look like your mother. Wonderful woman, I'm told. I wish I could have known her."

"Ah, thank you?" Laura said. "Forgive me, but have we met?"

"Not officially until right now," the woman said happily. Her kind eyes had small lines at the corners from years of big smiles. Laura had to guess she was in her fifties. "I'm Roberta. Your father's lady friend."

Laura's eyes shot wide. But before she could say anything, the woman yanked her in for another hug.

"He is just tickled to death that you're back in town!" Again she released Laura but kept a tight hold on her arm. "Me and my Lusty Ladies group was going to come down to the flower shop next week to welcome you properly, but when I got wind that you'd be here tonight, I just couldn't wait. Do you like coconut?"

Laura worked double time to process all the information and questions Roberta had thrown at her. First, her father was pushing seventy and dating this woman who . . . sure, seemed nice, but wasn't his type. Or was she? Hell, she had no idea! But between the leopard print, the bosom, and the suffocating hugs, she had to find her brain. Because Roberta clearly knew about her, the flower shop, and—

"Forgive me, did you say Lusty Ladies group?"

"Yes!" Roberta pulled her in like she was telling a secret. "My friends and I read all those dirty romance novels and such and talk about it. It's like a book club, only the steamier the better." She winked. "We're starting a new series next week. Cowboy with kink. Esther is bringing Chex Mix, and there's always wine."

Okay, Laura was officially lost somewhere between *cowboy*, *kink*, and *trail mix*. But one thing was certain, Roberta was . . . nice. Eccentric and chatty, but genuinely nice. Laura realized she hadn't gotten a minute to process that her father was even dating, much less going to live with this woman—oh, and he'd sold the house—and now, it was all hitting at once. But she couldn't bring herself to dislike Roberta. She wanted her father happy and, well, Roberta seemed at the very least that she could match his crazy, so that was a plus.

"I don't think I'll have time for a book club, but I appreciate the offer," Laura said with a smile, trying to be polite.

"Oh, of course! You're going to be so busy with that shop. Your father said you're setting to improve it! Sell flowers and all. That's great."

Her dad was talking about her? That made her smile. It also gave her hope that this next month would go well since her father already seemed to be spouting his faith in her to others. Jake could take note of that. She could make this work. And she would.

Roberta got a ping on her phone and giggled as she read the text message.

"I have to get going—that's your father now. His ears must have been burning." She smiled. "And he sure knows how to text sexy and this is a code red."

Ew! Laura could have lived the rest of her life not knowing that her father was apparently skilled at sexting.

45

"My shop is just a couple doors down," Roberta called loudly as she grabbed her leather jacket of the back of a bar stool and waved. "You come see me, we'll chat more!"

Roberta left and Laura realized her father had a more active sex life than she did. Which gave her the creeps, and now that drink she needed would have to be a double.

She made her way to the counter where, thank heaven, Hannah read her mind. A double vodka cranberry was waiting with a cherry floating on top.

"First time meeting your new stepmom, eh?" Hannah joked.

Laura finally shimmied her way between two older men, both in worn Carhartt jeans being held up by suspenders and smelling of saw-dust and salt water. Coastal men through and through.

She smiled at the bald one to her left. He just stared like she was a different life form. So she tried the gentleman on her right. He had to be pushing seventy and sported a gray beard down to his chest. The option of making friends didn't look promising.

She returned her attention to Hannah. "Yeah, I guess." She took several hearty swallows of her drink.

"Well, gear up for a homecoming there, Queenie, because everyone is excited to see you."

"Everyone?" Laura asked. And she missed how her best friend called her Queenie. Hannah had been the emo goth girl, total opposite of Laura, and yet they'd always been best friends.

"Yep. Your daddy's been talking about you coming home to anyone who will listen."

"Clearly," Laura said around another swallow, replaying the ambush she'd just encountered with Roberta.

"And everyone is excited to see how the small-town girl became the big-city woman and is back to take over Baughman."

Laura laughed at Hannah's flair for dramatics. It wasn't as glamor-ous as that, and yet, Hannah always made Laura feel like she was more than another plain Jane. Sure, she'd been prom queen, but Laura had never felt like more than an average girl riding around on a float made of toilet paper. It was also why she was always chasing big, exciting things, because deep down, she worried she wasn't exciting. Even her husband had grown tired of her. She'd allowed misery so long. But she was trying. Trying to stay. Trying to start fresh.

"Baughman?" Gandalf the Gray sitting next to her said abrasively and just looked at her, perplexed. "You're Walt Baughman's little girl?"

"Yes, that's right." Laura replied.

"So you're running the shop now?" Gandalf asked.

Laura blinked and her mouth went dry. Wasn't that the question of the day? She wasn't running it, exactly. But she wasn't about to spill the details to Gandalf here about how her father had given her a month to get along with Jake and make the flower shop a success before he'd intervene and pick a *real* boss.

Since she'd just shown up, and with the way everyone seemed to be eyeing her, her status as Walt's daughter wasn't a secret. The little flower shop was no longer that, though. It was a big operation with big machinery and big piles of supplies. But it was time for Laura to take what was hers and be proud. Only then could she make a name for herself in the town and sell her flowers. Not rocks and dirt like Jake. She had to set herself apart now if she'd ever be taken seriously and as her own person. Not the business. Not Jacob Lock's sidekick. Nope, she was in charge of the flower shop. Time she owned it.

"I'm the owner and will be working at the shop as well," she answered, feeling confident in that. Because she was ready to turn the flower shop around and oversee it. She just had to deal with Jacob Lock and how he'd been working in the warehouse for an eternity. "I'm going to revamp the floral shop," she finished.

Hannah nodded in support while shaking a martini. But Gandalf just humphed at her.

"I thought that the shop mostly did gravel and lumber or construction-type supplies."

"It was originally a floral shop," she said. Granted, it had been turned into a home-and-garden store several years ago, as it turned out. And now, of course, it was a warehouse monstrosity of resources on a large scale. "I'm getting the shop back to its roots."

"Ha-ha, pun intended?" Hannah said.

Laura smiled. "Yes!"

It was nice talking with someone who actually had a kind word for her. And seemed to be as excited as she was.

"This town doesn't have a flower shop, you know. Since your dad stopped selling, everyone has to go to Lincoln City," Hannah said with a wink. "You can corner the market."

"That's the hope," Laura said. A twinge of excitement raced through her.

"Yeah, I've had to look around for flower crap and arrangements or whatever the hell they're called, and it's annoying going all that way."

"You're looking for flowers? For an event?" Laura asked. "You didn't tell me about this."

"It just came up this morning," Hannah said, plopping a lime wedge in a Corona and sliding it down the bar to a random man. "My boss is dumping the planning for this event on me. It's this party—"

"Can I get shot of Jack over here, Hannah!" a man yelled from down the bar. Hannah wiped her hands on her apron and nodded.

"Duty calls," she said to Laura. "We'll talk more later, but enjoy your admirers . . ." Hannah gave a wink that made Laura wonder what the hell she was talking about. With a devious smile, she scooted down to wait on the other customers.

Laura stood with her drink in hand to find a table. When she turned around, she was met with a wall of man and effectively spilled her pink drink down the front of . . . *oh God* . . . a police uniform.

"I'm so, so sorry," Laura said, swiping at the stained chest now right in her face. The shiny badge and name tag read CLEARY.

Laura frowned up at him.

"Cleary? Gabe Cleary?"

She was met with dark eyes and the same blond-haired, boy-next-door smile she remembered from ten years ago.

"Welcome back, Laura. I see you're as graceful as ever."

Laura laughed, and he hugged her. She hugged him back. They'd been good friends back in school, and she patted his back platonically. He was holding on tighter, though, giving a gentle squeeze before releasing her. Gabe hadn't changed much. He'd been the quarterback of the football team and her prom date back then. Even though they'd never dated. And today he was an officer of the law and still looked the part of all-American guy.

"You look amazing," he said, standing back to look her over.

"Thank you, and you . . . are the sheriff?"

"Deputy. Old Bill Sandoval is still running the town, but he's set to retire soon."

She nodded. "Wow, that's great. So how are you?"

"I'm good. And you? Married? Babies?"

Laura laughed, and it was more awkward than humorous, so she had to take a drink of her half-spilled vodka.

"No, I'm divorced. No kids."

He nodded. "Living back here for a bit?"

"More like long-term."

"Well, then, I should take you to dinner," he said instantly. He pulled out his phone, and before Laura could think of her no-dating rule, she gave him her number. But she had to make sure expectations were clear.

"Dinner with a friend sounds nice," she said, emphasizing the *friend* part.

Gabe smiled and put his phone back in his pocket. "Yep, that line didn't change, either. Made me chase you back then, and I see I'm still in the friend zone."

The way he looked at her made her think Gabe had a mind to change that. But boy, she didn't not need that right now, especially since a pair of blue eyes were staring her down from the corner of the bar.

Jake Lock.

She didn't know when he'd come in, but he didn't take his eyes off her from across the room.

"I was just going to sit," Laura said, hoping to put some distance between her and Gabe and his flirty smile. Crap. Flirting was bad. He took a step in her direction as if joining her uninvited, but the radio on his uniform went off.

"Copy that," Gabe said into the radio on his shoulder. "I've got to run out."

"Serving and protecting," Laura said in understanding.

He kissed her cheeks and squeezed her hand. "I'm glad you're back. It's been a long time." He let her hand fall, and Laura couldn't shake the look in his eyes. Like there was a lot more Gabe wanted to say to her. But her capacity for handling men tonight was maxed out. "I'll call you," he said loudly as he left, and Laura's cheeks heated.

This was not good. Especially since she wasn't dating and she didn't owe explanations to anyone, but she had to get away from the scrutiny of Jake's gaze.

Laura moved to a small table near the corner. At least this way, no one was openly staring anymore and she could hide in the shadows a bit.

When she glanced around, she realized that most of the patrons were friendly and enjoying themselves.

Tipping back her glass, she drank down her mixed drink in record time.

Hannah nodded at her from across the room, and Laura nodded back, holding up her empty glass. She was going to need a few more before she not only felt the overwhelming chaos of today fade, but the chilling heat Jacob left behind earlier today disappear.

❧

Jake had walked into the bar ten minutes ago, and the first thing he'd seen was Deputy Gabe making moves on Laura. Figured. Thank God he saw his buddy Cal sitting on the corner stool so he could do his best to stay interested in what Cal was saying instead of staring Laura down.

Gabe had kissed her cheek. Which pissed Jake off. He'd felt her skin beneath his lips. Where Jake had been so damn close to her heat he could still feel it. And good thing Gabe had left when he had—Jake was ready to go over there and be a nuisance because he was . . . well, he wasn't jealous. Hell, he'd outgrown Gabe years ago. But this wasn't about size or build or the fact that Gabe had been captain of the football team once upon a time. He was just curious, was all. Because hadn't Laura just said that she wasn't dating? Did that include not dating Gabe? Because yeah, he'd heard her give him her number.

"Took you long enough," Cal said, sliding him a beer just as Jake sat down.

"Sorry, got held up." By held up, he meant that he'd stared down a super-sexy, super-pissed-off Miss Baughman in nothing but a towel and he'd needed a few minutes to recover from that experience. But he'd made it. And Friday night or not, it was business as usual. Because Cal wasn't just his friend, he was on the board of Custom Cabin Construction and the main manager on the ground who was oversee-ing the building of a new subdivision of log cabins.

"Still looking for a lumber supplier," Cal said.

"I haven't even taken a drink of my beer yet and already you're after me again?" Jake asked.

"I just don't get your problem, Lock. This is major money and a major project I'm throwing at you. And you keep giving me the brush-off."

"I'm not brushing you off, I'm telling you no."

"You have a thing against money and success?" Cal asked.

"Not at all. I just know my business. And while I'd love to be your lumber supplier, your big subdivision endeavor would tie up supplies and manpower for the next six months. I already have a customer base, and I can't take away from them."

"Then expand! Hire more people, order more lumber. I want you on my team."

"It's not that simple and you know it." And judging by the look on his friend's face, yeah, he did know it. Jake had a good thing going with the business. But Yachats was a small town. It wasn't like he could hire someone to take his place tomorrow and more men to oversee all the work. "And I won't leave Baughman."

"Yeah, no shit. You're never going to leave that place. This is the chance to work on something that's yours. Has your name on it. And you're staying at Baughman. It's six months. And I have steady contracts. Come be the foreman for yourself."

"It's still your gig," Jake said.

"Our gig. I'm the architect. You're the hands. This is your baby if you want it."

"I don't," Jake said. Sure, the idea of something for himself was appealing. But he loved Walt and Baughman, and the warehouse was his baby because he'd built it that way. He just didn't have the last name Baughman . . .

"I'm still holding out for you," Cal said. "I have time. I just need you to see reason."

Jake shook his head and smiled. His buddy had been captain of the debate team back in the day and had a knack for getting his way. But Jake was set in his decision. The smart move was to keep the business he had. Stable. Successful. Reliable. He didn't need to compromise that. And he didn't need to outsource his job at Baughman to take six months off to work on this new endeavor. Especially since Walt was looking to retire for real. Jake needed to be there to take over.

Solid, steady wins the race. No flashy, no crazy, no risk.

He glanced at Laura.

"So you going to tell me how that's going?" Cal said, gesturing over his shoulder toward Laura.

"Nothing to tell."

"Uh-huh. You forget how long we've been friends. You practically doodled her name in your high school notebook."

"Did not."

"And now she's your boss."

"She is not my boss. She's back in town running the flower shop," Jake said.

"Not what she was spouting off earlier. She was telling Russ over there that she was the owner."

What? There was no way that was true. Walt had just told them both they had a month to prove who'd be a better owner. Jake had a feeling this was Laura taking *initiative* in giving herself a new title. One she hadn't earned. That kind of brazenness was exactly what Jake stayed away from. Nothing sure and steady about that woman. So why was he still thinking about her skin?

Cal drained the last of his beer and smacked Jake on the shoulder. "Well, whatever is going on, here comes Russ, and word travels fast around here."

"Thanks a lot," Jake grumbled. Russ was a regular and a bigger gossip than the women in this town. But you'd never know from looking at the bearded logger.

"You're still in charge over at Baughman, right?" Russ asked Jake, coming to sit next to him. Man, did everyone want to grill him about the shop? The old man paused only to spit into his dip cup. "'Cause

Walt's daughter is back in town, and word is, she's taking over the business."

"I'm aware," Jake said, almost groaning at just how aware he really was of the mouthy blonde. After staring her down in a towel, followed by a cold shower of his own, he was still strung out on adrenaline and lust for her.

"So you're sure about the business?" Russ asked again.

Jake didn't want to go into details with Russ, or anyone else for that matter. But he replied, "I can assure you, I'm handling things. She's taking over the flower shop, but I'm still head foreman."

Russ nodded. "Think she'll go back to where she came from?"

Jake didn't know how to answer that. Would she stay long-term like she was talking about? Did he want that? Some things would be easier if she didn't, but Jake also wanted her around. Maybe he was delusional and wanted that shot with her he wished he'd taken in high school. Maybe he was just delusional, period.

In the meantime she claimed to be staying. Sure, they had a month to figure out the details and let Walt decide from there what to do. So until then, Jake had to figure out how he was going to survive. But all he could think about was another chance with Laura. Minus the towel.

Russ shook his head. "I gotta tell you that I don't feel comfortable doing business with her. I don't know her. She's Walt's kin, but judging by the looks of her?" Russ shook his head.

"What do you mean, 'judging by the looks of her'?" Jake tried to tamp down the slight flare of anger. Listening to Russ give Laura shit and threatening to pull his business based on judgment alone irritated him. But wasn't that what he was doing to her? Judging her before giving her a shot?

No, it was different—it had to be. Jake knew enough to know there was a chance Laura would go running after realizing that a lot went into Baughman and that it wasn't a dainty flower shop anymore. The flower shop was essentially dead, with no income, much less profit. She wasn't built for this kind of town or this kind of work. She had ambition and was the kind of risk Jake knew better than to take. The one time he'd risked before, he'd gotten burned. Badly. And it was on a woman just like her. Always wanting bigger and better things. Not a single pair of shoes aside from running ones.

Jake glanced again at Laura. She was hidden in the shadows a bit. He could barely tell it was her until he saw those bright brown eyes and a flash of her heels peeking out from under the table.

Fire-engine red and sexy as hell.

Yep, those weren't exactly root-settin' shoes. But there was a God in heaven, because she was looking straight at him. Not in a way one would an enemy, but the way a woman would look at a man. A man she was interested in.

He thought quickly how her body had trembled just at his nearness earlier. How she'd clearly been neglected in the bedroom department and how Jake wanted real bad to show her exactly how she should be treated.

Never one to leave a lady in need, Jake got up, left Russ where he was, and made the long walk across the bar to the beacon that was calling him. He was still several steps away when those pretty eyes of hers finally unfastened from his hips and landed on his face. Didn't last long, though, because she scanned his entire body before frowning and turning her attention back to her empty glass.

The prom queen just got caught checking him out. The thought made Jake swell with pride, and most of that lust from earlier he'd just gotten under control redoubled.

"Is there somewhere I can avoid you in peace?" she asked when he reached the table.

"Avoid? If memory serves, you're the one who stomped into my town, my warehouse, and then my *actual* house."

She bit her lip and twirled her delicate fingers around her glass. "Well, you're the one who came over here, so . . ."

"That's because you wanted me to."

"I did no such thing."

Jake rested his palm on the table edge and leaned down. "Yes, you did. Those pretty eyes of yours were scanning my entire body while you worked that lower lip nearly raw." He ran his free thumb over said lip and she gasped. "What was it you were thinking so hard about, I wonder?"

"How to get rid of you," she said, but there was an edge to her voice that made Jake's skin prick. Okay, he could play this game. Competition was one thing, but Laura was frustrated, in more ways than one. And he may not be high on her let's-be-buds list, but he was going to try to at least indulge her however she'd let him.

"How to get rid of my clothes, maybe," he countered. "You're not discreet when it comes to things you need."

"What I need is a key to the flower shop, which you still haven't given me."

"That's not all you need."

She pursed her lips and looked up at him. "And I'm sure you're going to tell me what it is I need now, huh?"

He gave her his best guaranteed-to-melt-panties grin and leaned a little closer until he could smell her neck. "I *felt* what you needed . . . right before you left my house."

The woman was hard up, that much was obvious. Maybe he was coming on strong, but he didn't care. Logic and reason left his mind when he was this close to her. All those bad ideas? Like the fact that she was his mentor's daughter and a flight risk? Didn't matter. She was also technically his competition and a pain in his ass, until Walt made a decision twenty-nine days and thirteen hours from now. But he wanted her. All that other important stuff fell second to that one fact.

Fantasies die hard, and Jake couldn't help but wonder if she still had her old cheerleading uniform . . .

"Didn't your mother teach you not to stare?" Laura said. And Jake realized he was doing just that.

"My mother taught me to appreciate women. Especially a fine one."

"Oh my God, was that another line?" she asked.

"That's just a fact."

This was a means to an end no matter how he swung it. Either she or he would take over at the end of the month. Walt was going to retire and name a head of the company. So Jake just had to do his best to show he was right for the job. Granted, her yelling at him in nothing more than a towel had been hot. And he'd be more than happy to witness that again. They responded to each other. And despite his better judgment, he could really use a night of getting lost. He was juggling a hell of a lot and just wanted to relax, preferably next to Laura Baughman.

"I know more about you than you'd like to think," he said. "I know that you haven't been here. And actions speak loud. Your actions have been in California, and mine have been here."

Her eyes shot wide and her throat worked double time to swallow what looked like a dose of concrete.

"You know nothing," she rasped.

"I know enough."

She leaned into him. "Then you know that I work very, very hard. I'm ruthless when it comes to what I want."

"So am I."

The heat passing between them was enough to tense Jake. He wanted to throttle this woman as much as he wanted to kiss her. He'd never wanted someone so much.

He leaned closer.

"Say the word and we can stop pretending. I know what you want," he said.

"I don't even like you," she said. Which was a lie. She liked him a little. He glanced at her teeth sinking into that plump bottom lip again.

"I was talking about the shop." He grinned. "But since you brought it up . . ."

"Get over yourself."

"I'd be happy to, just as soon as you admit that you want to get under me."

"You're out of your mind."

He shrugged. "I can read women. Especially ones that wear their emotions like you do."

"Oh yeah? Then you can read this pretty well?" When she displayed her middle finger, he had to hold back a chuckle. She was raw fire and passion and frustration.

"I hear you own the shop," he said, backpedaling to his earlier comment.

A look of guilt flashed across her face. "I'm just trying to establish my place here."

"I get that," Jake said. And he did. "But I'm in this, too. Baughman is important to me."

"I know."

"Then we either need to work together, or—"

"Or realize that I will inherit everything and I want what's best for the business," she said confidently.

"Oh, you will, huh?" Jake countered, a flare of anger hitting him. "I could always buy you out. Even if your father gave you everything. Which I doubt."

"Never."

"Why?"

"Because the flower shop is already mine."

"I'm not trying to take anything away from you."

"But you won't work with me."

"I won't put the business in jeopardy, and I won't finance your flower shop makeover with money the warehouse has earned."

"I know that you're this son my father never had, but I'm going to make him . . ." She trailed off, and Jake frowned. She was going to make him what? Surely she couldn't mean proud? She had to know that Walt was already proud of her.

"Well, my offer stands," he said and deliberately scanned her body. She noticed, and he liked how much it pissed her off. Almost as much as it did him, because he didn't want to want her. "On all accounts."

"Again. I don't even like you."

"You don't have to like me to need me."

"Oh, now I *need* you."

"Yes, you do." He'd go another route with this if he had to. Because she was stubborn and gambling with Walt's and his life's work. However he had to wear her down, he would. Because he refused to let the business suffer. "For your professional sake, if not your personal sake." He paused to take a good, hearty view of those amazing breasts, which—judging by the beading nipples showing through her silky shirt—were still a bit cold. Or turned on.

She swallowed hard, and his eyes were riveted to the action. Was she technically his competition for the business? Yes. The enemy? Sure. But she was also prime, ready, and sexy as sin.

"You honestly think I could use you professionally?" she scoffed. "I'm a professional. In marketing." She spoke extra slowly, like he was an idiot. "You don't even open the whole store on a weekday."

She was stuck on this flower shop. Again. "I told you once, you want to open the floral shop, be my guest. Just don't come crying to me when you have no idea what you're doing with orders or sit there surrounded by crickets. But you know where to find me—in the warehouse, where the real money is made."

She chewed on her lip a little. "Working together would be . . ."

"Frustrating?" he finished for her.

"Extremely," she agreed and looked over his chest again. Yeah, they might hate each other, but deep down, she wanted him. Just like he wanted her. And they both knew it. Didn't mean it was a good idea. Hell, it was a terrible idea.

"Okay, Jacob, I'll play your little game of hypothetical. Let's say you're right," she said. "Suppose I want you. Personally and professionally."

"Need," he corrected. "And I am right."

"What is it you propose? We . . . what?" She wiggled her eyebrows and in a mocking tone said, "Fool around?" She smiled, but not in a humorous way. "Then what? We'd work together? Be friends? Forget that there isn't this competition between us and we really want each other gone?"

"Actually, working together would benefit you more than me." There were several things he wanted to address from her last statement, but he'd start there. "In a small town, personal relationships matter. Everyone has worked with me, knows me. That goes a long way around here."

He looked at her lips, thinking of how good they must feel. How badly he wanted to taste them. How much he was kicking himself for not doing so earlier. Which brought him to his next point. "And no, we wouldn't *fool around*, then be friends. I'd fuck you until you moaned my name, make you come over and over until you couldn't take it anymore. Oh, and the competition would absolutely *not* be forgotten."

That lush mouth he'd been thinking about parted on a shocked breath. She stood up, making her tight body brush against his, and faced him.

"You don't sugarcoat anything, do you?"

He really wanted to tell her he'd happily sugarcoat her, but instead he went with, "I like to make things clear up front, especially when it comes to building expectations. But it's always understood that I deliver on what I promise. That's just good business."

He winked.

She huffed.

"I don't think I'll have any problem building personal relationships with customers."

He arched a brow. "Oh, really? Then why was Russ Paxton talking to me about backing out of the gravel order he has coming in from us? He gets gravel every quarter. That's a large chunk of steady income for the business, all because he's not sure about dealing with *you*."

"You mean Gandalf over there?"

Jake nodded. "He owns Paxton Landscaping and is the largest business in four counties. He's also one of our biggest customers." He leaned in a little until her breasts pressed against his chest and he had her sandwiched between his body and the edge of the table. "Still certain about your interpersonal skills?"

She glanced over his shoulder in the direction of Russ, and judging by those wide brown eyes, no, she wasn't certain.

"I don't want to lose customers," she said quietly. So quietly, in fact, Jake wasn't sure she was aware she'd said it out loud. Did she actually care about the business? "What would I have to do to"—she flicked her wrist, motioning to the expanse of the bar—"fit in better?"

"Well . . ." He shifted his hips, causing his hard cock to drag across her flat stomach. The little moan she gave was the green light he was looking for. She could deny it all she wanted, but want him she did. "You and me showing a unified front would be a start."

She nodded, her eyes staring at his mouth. "Unified front?"

"I'd be happy to help you. Just say the word."

Her eyes flashed with something dark and hot. "Help me personally or professionally?"

He grinned. "Both. We can start by talking over dinner tomorrow." He was trying really hard to be a gentleman and at least feed her, talk to her, and have a nice evening with her before doing what he really wanted to do, which was hit his knees and bury his face between those slick thighs of hers.

She glanced down at where their lower halves met. Their bodies knew exactly what to do. He just needed a little bit of privacy and a hard surface and he'd be happy to swap pent-up aggression for sex with Miss Baughman. He glanced at the table right behind her and was instantly reevaluating how necessary privacy was.

Trailing her finger along his belt, she rose just enough to brush her lips against his and whispered, "You're forgetting something, Jacob . . . I'm not going to date you. And I think I can handle *both* my needs on my own."

Jake's eyes snapped open, but she had already stepped around him and was heading out the door.

"I never said anything about dating," he called after her.

Laura was damn near running in her last pair of heels, scuffing them to hell, down the long dirt road that led to her camper.

Yes, she had driven, but it was only a mile away and she'd had a couple of drinks. She didn't want to risk anything the way her head was feeling. Which was more from Jake than from the alcohol, but still. She needed the air.

The night breeze was cold, but it did nothing to stifle the heat in her blood or on her skin. She'd almost kissed Jacob Lock! Actually, she'd almost done a lot more than that. She had been ready to hop up on the table, spread her legs, and take him up on his offer.

The man was annoying and getting under her skin in more ways that she'd like. He was not the shy boy she remembered. He was all man. Spoke, walked, and smelled like one. Like sex. Because the more time she'd spent around him—in town, even—the more she was wondering what was happening. But her goal wouldn't change. The flower shop mattered. Mattered to her. Mattered to her mother once upon a time. And it was all she had left of her. She would not only make this place her home, she'd make it a success.

First she just needed to get out of these first twenty-four hours. Emotions were weighing hard. Like she could feel the pressure of all these internal questions, fears, and insecurities surrounding her like a heavy blanket, humming with building tension.

Her head was in shambles and her heart was aching. She'd give just about anything to take out some aggression on something . . . or someone.

Those pieces of her life she was trying to round up were slipping between her fingers. How could one person hurt her feelings, then turn her on, then make her feel like a part of his team, all in one conversation?

She had to get control. She was in charge now. Taking back her life. Her future. Jacob was separate. And she had to woman up and deal with him or stay away from him. Either way, she definitely wasn't dating him. His presence was too much. Too engulfing.

I'm in trouble . . .

Because he was right. She did want him so bad, to a point of need. Her body was betraying her with every brush of his skin or flash of his grin. She had a feeling Jacob Lock could live up to his promises . . . or threats. His hands and mouth alone could do amazing things in record time. That much she was fairly certain of.

So she'd have to fight harder. Because the moment she was still, she just might start thinking about how much her father loved him, had built with him, shared with him. While she was in California. She'd missed out. And she'd lost big.

She kicked the gravel and cursed.

The sneaky topic of hate screwing crept into her brain again, and she shook it away. She would love to physically take out her feelings on Jacob. And they wouldn't be the warm and fuzzy kind.

He'd made her gasp, just from the nearness of him earlier. But he had said he could make her moan. Part of her wanted him to try. And that part of her needed to shut up, because she was trying to run a business, which was shaping up to be a lot more difficult that she'd anticipated. Reputation mattered. And she didn't have much of one, which could be bad for Baughman. And she'd be damned if that company did anything less than thrive under her watch.

But taking Jake up on his offer of help?

"Not smart," she said out loud. Because she needed to hear it—to accept it.

Lights came up behind her, paired with big tires rolling on the dirt road. She didn't need to look back to know it was Jake in his truck, coming her way.

He rolled down the passenger window and slowed his Chevy to keep pace with her strides.

"What the hell are you doing? You could get lost or—"

"I'm fine," she said, attempting to maintain the hustle. He pulled ahead, put his truck in park, rounded the front, and headed her off by the tailgate.

"You can't just leave like that," he said. With the tailgate at his back, Jacob Lock and a two-ton diesel were blocking her path.

"What do you care?" she said. "Isn't this part of your grand plan?"

She stepped toward him. The truck was off, but the lights remained on. Between that and the moonlight, she could see his blue eyes blazing on the otherwise desolate road.

"My plan is to alleviate whatever the hell is between us and make sure the business doesn't go under in the meantime."

She crossed her arms over her chest. "I am educated in marketing. It's my plan to make sure the business has its best year yet. I just need—"

"Oh, I know what you need," he said. "You're just too stubborn to admit it."

Her gaze snapped to his. The dam had broken. She had been struggling with herself for a long time, but more recently, struggling with Jacob Lock. Fine. She could play. She could show him exactly the kind of woman she was capable of being. The kind of woman she wanted to be. She was done being overlooked or underestimated.

"You want to push me?" Using her pointer finger, she tapped his hard chest, emphasizing her words. "You want to make me go crazy? Make me *need* you?" She tapped his chest again, and his back thumped against the tailgate.

A low growl broke in his throat, but his eyes stayed on her face. He was letting her touch him, glare at him, push his buttons. He was much stronger and more solid than she was—but he was letting her come at him.

It was then she realized how badly she wanted to get lost. In him. With him. The one man who understood more about her father she did. The one man deemed better than her, yet how he'd pushed her. Was pushing her. As if the challenge was what she needed.

All of the grief, confusion, anger, and lust boiled over. She was tired of pushing him—tonight she would pull.

The last rational thought left her mind. She fisted his shirt and yanked him toward her until his mouth crashed down on hers. She kissed him hard, with all the anger she felt. She should hate him—kind of did hate him, actually. But she would show him how wrong he was. She didn't need him. Not for anything personally or professionally.

Keeping her mouth on his, she pushed him back farther against the tailgate and drove her tongue into his mouth. He tasted like beer and lime and so good. It was everything she could do to stop from drinking him down whole.

His big hands landed heavy on her ass and hoisted her up. She instantly wrapped her legs around his hips.

"You're a wild little thing, aren't you?" he rasped against her mouth. With her in his arms, he turned so that her back was now against the truck.

"There's nothing nice about this, you understand?" she said, driving her fingers into his hair and kissing down his neck, throwing in a few bites along the way.

"Yes, ma'am," he said, tugging the front of her shirt down until she heard a rip and the cool night air skated across her bare breasts. "You want rough and dirty?" He lifted her up just a little higher so his mouth was in line with her breasts. "I can do that."

And he did.

He latched on to one nipple, and Laura threw her head back and gasped to the sky. Stretching her arms across the edge of the tailgate, she opened herself up for more of his attention. Arching into his mouth as he laved at her, sucking hard, licking and biting. He devoured her breasts like they were covered in candy. The raw ferociousness of his mouth was nothing she'd ever felt. Like he had to taste more of her. Pull more into his mouth. Her entire core ached with emptiness. She was tired of that ache. Tired of being alone.

Not tonight.

Tonight she'd take her fill, because everything would be different tomorrow. Everything would be back to the competition and the business. But tonight? She pulled him closer. She wasn't giving him up. She would take full advantage and deal with the fallout later.

Right now, she was busy showing how much she didn't need him.

She lifted his shirt up over his head and he raised his arms, gladly letting her.

"Good Lord," she gasped when she saw his rock-hard chest and abs. Muscles like those didn't come from a gym—they came from day after day of manual labor.

"Impressed?" he asked with all the confidence in the world. She didn't need to answer; they both knew she was drooling.

"Muscles or not, you have yet to make me moan. I thought you were a man of your word and always delivered, Lock."

That made his blue eyes icy with intent, and a wicked grin split his face. Without warning, he spun her around. Her bare breasts pressed into the cold metal of his truck, the shock making her skin buzz and light up in the most delicious way. She may have cold metal against her front, but she had solid man, radiating heat, flush against her back.

"That mouth of yours is going to be begging here in a minute," he rasped in her ear, then bit down hard on the lobe. He unbuttoned her pants and removed them.

Gripping the back of her thigh, he dragged her foot to rest on the bumper of his truck.

"Almighty," he said. She glanced over her shoulder and saw him staring between her legs. She waxed regularly, and apparently Jake liked that.

"Are you impressed?" she asked with the same confidence he'd dished out only a moment ago.

He met her stare and there was a predatory gleam in his eyes that made her shiver.

"No . . . I'm *starving*."

He bent and in one fast swoop fastened his mouth against her core.

"Oh yes!" She gripped the truck and held on as Jake drove his tongue into her hot depths over and over, only to come up to suck on her clit, sparking fire beneath every square inch of skin. "Yes, oh, Jake, right there." She tried to move, to meet his seeking mouth, but he set the pace and ate at her with a wild passion, exactly how he wanted. She was on the brink, stars twinkling behind her eyes . . . so close . . .

He stopped and rose.

She slammed her hand against the truck. "No! I was—"

"You ready to beg for it?" he asked and slapped her ass. To her surprise, she moaned. "Ah, there's that moan. Granted, hearing you scream to the sky was also nice."

"Not nice," she shot out. Her chest was heaving, trying to catch up to her lungs, which were working overtime. The thwarted orgasm she'd been on the brink of only fueled the anger and need she felt toward him.

She heard his zipper come down, then a rip of cellophane.

"I'm still waiting for that pretty mouth of yours to beg . . ." His big, callused hand squeezed her ass as he came right behind her and positioned himself at her entrance. The crown nudged her core but he held, not breaching her until he got what he wanted.

But she wouldn't. She was still not needing him.

Proving strength. Faking it. Whatever she was doing, she was dying. She just needed to feel him. But she wouldn't give in. She'd win. All of this. She'd win. Because if she didn't, she just might have to start wondering how little there was left of her heart.

"Either get on with it or don't, Jake. I won't beg."

With a satisfied groan, he thrust deep.

"Oh!" she gasped. He took her completely. Stretching and filling her to the hilt.

"Stubborn woman." He thrust again. "But damn, you feel so good." He stirred his hips. "So tight and wet." He pulled out, then returned with another punishing thrust. Her head lolled back and rested against his shoulder. "You don't wanna beg? Fine. But you'll talk." He hammered in and out harder. "How long have you been wet for me?"

With one hand clamping her side, he pumped again and again. His hips slapped her ass, filling the quiet night with the sounds of their skin meeting and echoing out into the darkness. When she didn't answer because she was too busy moaning and chanting his name, he snaked the other arm around, between her breasts, to cup her throat.

"How. Long. Laura?" he said with a sharp bite to his words. "How long have you been wet for me?"

"S-since I first saw you," she admitted. She'd tell him anything if it meant he'd keep going. Take her over the edge and let her lose herself in the pleasure he was unleashing.

"Good," he growled, fucking her slow and hard. Each thrust pressing her bare breasts farther into the cold tailgate while she was being burned up from the inside out. "Because I've been hard for you all damn day."

He pumped again, but he held her tight. His arms like a vise around her, but his palm gentle on her neck. Like he was capable of being rough and soft all at the same time. She loved the feeling of being totally dominated by him. Wrapped up in his strength, taken like a wild animal, craving nothing beyond his touch.

She'd never felt more primal. Never been taken over by passion, by lust, like this before. She was getting closer. That fire he'd built up with his mouth on her sensitive flesh flooded.

"Yes . . . yes . . . Jake, yes!"

But he stilled. Buried deep inside her and not moving. Taking her to the edge only to keep her there. She groaned a frustrated breath, and his deep chuckle in her ear ignited her skin another degree.

"Still hate me?" he asked.

"Right now?" She wiggled her hips, attempting to get a little friction to finish the job, but he held her immobile. "Urg! Yes! I hate you so much right now!"

She felt his smile against her hair; then he shifted his hips, hitting even deeper than she thought possible, and sent her careening over the edge of bliss.

She screamed. His name? The Lord's name? She didn't know. All she knew was that her vision wavered from the intensity of the pleasure. Hot, pulsing lava replaced her blood, and her heart beat it out a mile a minute. Just when she thought she couldn't take any more, his cock hardened further, and he hissed when she felt him twitch with his own release. It was so powerful, it made her come again before the first orgasm subsided.

They stayed like that for a long moment—her head against his chest, his arms wrapped around her. She gently kissed his neck as he stayed inside her, as if unwilling to leave her body. Before she realized what a sweet gesture it was, she looked up at him.

"This doesn't change anything," she said.

He met her stare. With her bare ass against him, one of her feet still on the bumper of his truck, he smiled down at her. "We'll see about that."

Chapter Four

Jake kicked his bedsheets off like a kid throwing a tantrum. He kind of was being a brat, though, because he hadn't slept in twenty-four hours. Not since Laura had walked into his life and he'd gotten a firsthand taste of her last night.

He needed to stop making a habit of getting into close quarters with her. Though it was a delightful habit, it was also a bad idea. Very, very bad. Because she tasted better than he could have ever imagined.

He was still reeling from last night, and the sun had been up for a couple of hours now. He'd watched the dark night fade to grays, and finally blue skies peeked through. Yep, it was a new day, but he still felt like he was in the eye of a tornado named Laura.

Last night, she had attempted to put up a fight about him taking her home, but her legs were wobbly and he'd like to think it was from him kissing the hell out of her. Or maybe fucking her against his truck.

Either way, he had given her a ride and seen her to the doorstep of her camper. After she'd slammed said door in his face, he'd walked the few paces to his own house. Not the happy good night he'd hoped for.

That woman made his head, and other parts of his body, ache.

He ran a hand through his bed-rumpled hair, padded the long, quiet steps to his kitchen, and poured a cup of coffee. The walls were bare, but he had a lot of windows and a nice view. Standing in any main room in the house, you could pretty much look out and see the expanse of land that surrounded him. Land and a camper, that was.

He took a long swallow of coffee and thought about sitting on his couch. Then didn't. Because the leather was cold this time of the morning. In fact, his house was cold all the time. Jeanine had left him before the house was fully built, so they never got to fight about the thermostat. They had also never fought about what to do with the spare room. Jake's vote had been for a nursery; Jeanine's vote had been to leave him for a better man in a better place. Big-city dreams with a big-city guy. That wasn't Jake. Never had been and wouldn't ever be.

Now he had a house for a life he didn't have. One that included love, happiness, and family. What he did have, though, were pieces of a busted heart and experience with women who constantly had their eye on something better.

Speaking of women always looking for something better, he glanced outside for the hundredth time at the bright morning and the trailer in his driveway. Was she awake yet? Why should he care? She wasn't dating him. Something she'd made very clear. And he wasn't backing off what was right for the business. Which was steadiness and no risk.

But goddamn, she was passionate.

Strong.

Stubborn as hell.

And she seemed to know exactly what she wanted.

Until something better came along . . .

Because Laura Baughman was ambitious. And that meant taking risks and opportunities, and to hell with the rest. She'd run once, might again, and Jake just had to be prepared for the latter. And while he shouldn't like her, he couldn't get last night out of his mind.

"Knock, knock!" a happy voice rang out. His sister, Erica, came through his front door, letting herself in like she always did. "It's past breakfast," she said, eyeing him. "Put on a shirt. I brought muffins."

He gave her a half hug and grabbed a muffin out of the little pastry box, not caring about the shirt at the moment, because his eyes were back on the trailer.

"You're here earlier than usual," he said. It was a Saturday, after all. And even though Erica came by every Saturday morning when she was off shift at the clinic, he'd never seen her before nine.

She walked in, her curly hair swinging way past her back. She had the same dark hair and blue eyes as Jake, but she looked just like their mother. Petite and always sweet, with a smile. Jake apparently looked like his dad. Big, tall, and rough around the edges. Something he hated knowing and being compared to since the man was a poor excuse for a father, husband, and general human being.

She poured herself a cup of coffee and leaned against the counter.

"Heard you had an interesting day yesterday," she said with a smile. "Wanted to come check on you a bit early. Get the scoop."

Seemed the small-town chatter mill was already in full swing. By now, most of Yachats would have heard that Laura Baughman was back and set to work in one of the most lucrative businesses in town. Though she was spinning it that she was an owner. Which was half-true and was already ruffling some feathers. He'd never finished his conversation with Russ last night, but he wasn't worried. Jake controlled the warehouse, and that was final.

"Day was fine," he said and took another bite of muffin.

"Fine?" Erica repeated, eyeing him. He may be the oldest, but Erica was sharp. She saw through his bullshit real quick. Always had. "Is that why you're so fidgety and keep staring at that god-awful monstrosity parked in your driveway?"

"Hey, that was Walt's."

"Yeah, and it looks condemned. Thank God he finally moved in with his lady."

"It's not condemned," he said. Sure it was rough, but it was livable. And Laura hadn't complained once, so that was something. Impressive, actually, considering he'd wager that her shoes were more expensive than Jake's whole wardrobe put together.

"You should get rid of it. Or at least hide it," Erica said.

Jake shook his head. Sure, everyone might know Laura was in town, but no one knew the details of her arrangement. Like that she was living in the old trailer in his driveway and drinking hose water. Wow—now that he thought about it, it sounded kind of bad.

The woman might irritate him, but he respected her drive. He just didn't understand how she could be so tenacious about taking over the shop and living in her dad's old camper when she had been used to the California city and sun the past ten years.

"I can't get rid of the camper," Jake said. He hadn't told his sister about Laura. Because, honestly, he hadn't had much time to think about it. But those red heels she wore were stomping all over his life.

"And I don't need to let anything go," he added. Because he was trying like hell to hang on, actually. Hang on to the business, and to his own sanity.

He glanced at the camper again.

The blonde holed up inside there was threatening both.

Erica looked around his home as if she were examining invisible wallpaper until finally her stare was serious when it landed back on him. Shit, he knew that look. She was scrutinizing. And any minute she was going to tell him exactly what she thought his problem was.

"I think you do need to take a look around," she said. "You have nothing in your home aside from functional basics, really, but you hold on to things you should be moving past. And I'm not just talking about the trailer."

He growled low and took a drink of coffee. Oh, he knew what she was talking about.

"I'm not in the mood for this, Erica."

"I just worry about you," she said and tucked a thick lock of hair behind her ear. When she did that and put her hand on her hip, she looked just like his mother when he was on the receiving end of a scolding. He knew she cared. It was why she came over every Saturday morning to make sure he was still alive and to feed him pastries.

He still felt the need to say, "I'm a grown man and I'm fine."

"I know you're *fine*," she said. "You're always *fine*. But fine isn't good, Jake. I worry about your emotions."

He laughed. "Well, I can honestly say that my emotions are fine, too. But thanks for the concern."

"Look around you," she said. "This place is—"

"This place is a beautiful home."

"It would be if you could call this a home. It's desolate. It's like you're living in a shell of a house. There's no sign of home anywhere in here."

"Well, sorry I don't decorate because it's unnecessary for me."

"It's not about picking out curtains, it's about actually living. Waking up and living a happy life. You just function. Go to work and come home. That's it."

"That's all I've ever done."

"That's not true," Erica said quickly. "You had a life, a happy one. At least you did before Jeanine left you."

That hit hard. She had left him a year ago, and it still hurt. He'd built this place to have this idea of home that his sister was currently shoving down his throat. A home with a wife and kids. All of which he'd mapped out in a future with Jeanine, only for her to leave for bigger and better things. Now he was the chump stuck with the house and no family to put in it.

Technically she'd left him while he was still in construction on the house. He remembered being so excited to tell her they'd finally gotten the drywall up and it was time to pick paint colors, only to find she'd had her bags packed. She'd taken his sense of trust, his dreams for the future, and the ring. Which was fine. She could have it. All of it.

Because Jake didn't need her for a future. Or paint colors. He had his place and a job he liked, and that's it.

He. Was. Fine.

She was a risk he shouldn't have taken in the first place. And he'd learned his lesson.

He glanced at the camper again.

Have I?

"I didn't mean that to sound so harsh," Erica said, backpedaling, because Jake realized it had been a solid minute and he still hadn't responded. "You used to smile more. Losing Jeanine was hard on you, I know. But you are so . . . predictable. All the time. I want you to be happy, truly happy again. You should get out more. Spend time with friends. Make new friends."

Oh, he'd made a new friend from an old friend last night. Seeing Laura in that moonlight had been a fantasy second to none. But she wasn't just a risk—she was a walking time bomb. Ready to blow up everything in a moment and leave a trail of bloody hearts in her wake.

"I'm stable and responsible because I'm running a business," he said.

"A business that's not yours," she countered.

"It basically is. I'm not trying to take over Walt's business to be greedy. I want it to thrive when he retires, and I care about the place and this town," he said. The thought of Laura crept into his mind again, reminding him just how much of a threat she was. City girl coming in, wanting bigger and better things and messing with everything he'd planned. Everything he'd promised Walt once upon a time. He'd taken Jake up on his idea to sell more home supplies but had insisted that the business stay local, stay true to the town and the people. And that's what Jake would see through. Because he wasn't going anywhere. He wished he could honestly believe the same about Laura.

No matter what, he couldn't let everything Baughman Home Goods had grown into perish.

"And what if Baughman Home Goods isn't going to be yours? What if Walt's daughter stays and keeps the business? The entire business?"

"She won't," Jake said. "She wants the flower shop and has thirty days to make just that work. Walt left it up to us how to deal with everything in that time."

He'd worked too hard with Walt to disappoint him. He wouldn't let the business go to Laura purely for the fact that she could damage it. Baughman Home Goods was a staple around town—as was Walt's reputation. He'd fight like hell to preserve both.

"And how's that going?"

Jake shrugged. So far, it was okay. Laura was talking a big game but not stepping on the toes of the business. Yet. But when he didn't say any of this out loud, his sister clearly caught that he was stalling and didn't want to discuss this further.

"Fine." His sister threw her hands up and let them slap down on the sides of her thighs. The sound echoed a bit, making Jake realize that maybe his place was a bit barren. "I don't want to argue about your business."

"Thank you," he said.

"But I do want to argue about your personal life."

Ah, Christ.

"Look, Jake, it's been a while since you dated. There's a lot of nice women down at the PTA that always ask me about you."

Here we go . . .

His sister may be younger than him and young in general, but she was the oldest twenty-six-year-old he knew. Because her life had been anything but easy. And normally, Jake wouldn't be turned off to dating, but the last year had been hell. Between Jeanine leaving and Walt taking up with his lady friend, Jake had poured every bit of energy he had into building the business to be stable and secure so Walt could live comfortably. No, dating hadn't been high on his priority list. But that had changed twenty-four hours ago. With a set of red heels and one prom queen with a sharp kiss and even sharper bite.

Who has a firm stance on not *dating . . .*

She might not be interested in dating him. But he was interested in getting her to scream his name again.

In fact, he was more interested in changing her no-dating policy. Maybe they could coexist and enjoy their time together? Make this business work between them. Win-win in the end? Maybe he was once again delusional, like Laura had said.

He just had to attempt to keep his dick in his pants in the meantime.

He shook his head. His sister bringing up dating was the last thing he needed right now. Time for a subject change.

"Speaking of the PTA, where are the kiddos?" he asked.

Erica had twin six-year-old girls, Bella and Lexi. She was an amazing mom. Especially since she was raising them on her own after their dad took off while she was still pregnant. Jake would always be there for her and his nieces. Unfortunately, his sister had taste like their mother, and both had gone for men who left them high and dry when things got tough.

Which was why Jake wouldn't ever leave here. It was home. His family and he loved it. Took care of them.

"They're at a playdate, which reminds me . . ." She glanced at her watch, then grabbed her cell out of her pocket. "I'm just going to call and check in." She started dialing and headed back to his room for privacy.

And just then, Jake saw the camper out front. A large smile split his face, because not only was Laura stirring, she was exiting . . . and coming his way.

Laura cleared her throat and gave a good tug to her crisp, white button-up, making sure it was securely tucked into her pressed black skirt. She was dressed for business, because she was a business owner, after all. And after a couple of years of working at her old marketing firm, business and business casual were the only clothes she had. Casual didn't fit in her world.

She clutched her legal pad against her chest and took a deep breath. She'd been up all night thinking of Jacob Lock. And that had only gotten her puffy eyes and a migraine. Oh, she also had a sizable bruise on her butt from where she'd been hammered into the tailgate . . . literally. But that soreness just made other aches more noticeable and turned her thoughts to Jacob Lock and all the power that came with him. Especially when he was hammering her.

Those kinds of thoughts needed to stop!

She had to focus. Not on his mouth or his muscles or the insane way he moved his hips. No, she had a business to focus on. A business he was trying to take from her. A business that she had ideas about.

And it was time she took charge.

In her best professional power outfit, she knocked on Jacob's door, ready to forget everything but the competition between them and to claim her place in this new life once and for all. She was not getting caught up in a man again. Sure, she'd had no idea sex or a man could be so amazing until last night . . . but she was not projecting her issues— thank you, therapy—and she was not chasing a man's approval. She was taking charge. And Jacob Lock wasn't on the agenda.

Last night was a slipup, but she'd keep to her no-dating rule, at the very least. A one-night stand didn't count as a date, so that was a good thing.

The heavy door opened, and so did her mouth when she took in the sight before her.

Jacob Lock with sexy bed hair, dark stubble, a sleepy smile, and low-slung pajama pants.

"Good morning, Miss Baughman. Sleep well?" With a cup of coffee in one hand, he raised his other to lean against the door frame, stretching that eight-pack of abs and making her instantly drool.

"Stop," she whispered.

He frowned. "Stop what?"

Stop looking sexy as sin!

But she couldn't very well scream that out. No matter how badly she wanted to. She looked at him, and all that gumption she'd worked up was out the window. She was going to tell him where he could go. Which was straight to her bed—

No! Hell. He could go to hell.

Maybe after a brief pit stop at her bed?

Okay, her conscience was a lusty bitch, and it was time for Laura to get a damn grip.

She cleared her throat and clutched tighter the drafts of ideas she'd drawn up the night before. It was the only thing that had kept her sane and off the Jacob sex topic.

"Good morning," she tried again, bypassing the whole *stop looking sexy* thing. Smooth. Really smooth. "Clearly, I woke you, and I apologize for the inconvenience."

Okay, her voice was better. Professional. So far, so good.

"You didn't wake me," he said with a grin.

She kept her train of thought as consistent as she could—but then he shifted his stance, making the thin gray material of his pants cling a little more in the right place, and suddenly her mind was in the gutter again. Oh, she knew exactly how well that man could move those hips. Especially when he was inside her—

"Stop," she whispered again. Thankfully, this time it was so quiet Jacob couldn't hear it. Not like she needed to give him a reason to think her crazy. She was already talking to herself. Wait . . . maybe she was crazy. No, just sleep deprived, surely. That's why she had a hard time thinking of much more than Jacob's body, or his mouth.

What was she doing again? Oh, right! Being assertive and running a business.

"I need the key for the floral shop," she announced proudly.

He took a sip of his coffee and eyed her. "It's Saturday."

"Yes, I can read a calendar. However, it is *my* shop, and I've decided to go in today and revive it."

"That right?" he said, amused. "Well, I think that's great, Laura."

She frowned. He was being nice to her. "You do?"

"Of course I do. It is your shop, as you said."

"Okay . . . thank you."

He nodded. Why was he trying to be nice to her?

"It's a shop of empty coolers. But don't worry, it'll look like a floral shop in no time. I think I can handle it."

"I'm sure you can. And I'll stick to the warehouse."

Ah, now she understood. He wanted to remind her that they were separate. Which Laura didn't agree with. The business was a business as a whole. And she wanted to be a part of it. Even the parts—like the warehouse—she didn't understand.

But the way Jake looked at her got her caught up. She could get lost in those ice-blue eyes.

No, she couldn't.

"The key?" she asked again.

When he turned to reach for the small table by the entrance, that impressive chest stretched farther, and good Lord, the man had muscles she hadn't thought existed on a body.

"Best of luck to you," he said and dropped the single silver key into her open palm.

"No luck required. I have skills—"

"I'm aware," he said with a wink. He was not helping her plan of being indifferent. Because every breath he took just made all that mocha skin flex a little more over those impressive pecs.

"Stop flirting with me," she said. "I'm trying to discuss business."

He raised his brows. "Well, then by all means. I'd love to talk business with you. Your shop versus my warehouse?"

"No," she said between gritted teeth. "I have some solid ideas of how to incorporate more business toward the floral shop." She patted her legal pad with pride. "While learning more about the warehouse and how it can play a part."

He glanced at said paper.

"So you were up all night fantasizing about something that isn't going to happen?" he said and looked her up and down with a heated gaze.

She lifted her chin. "So were you," she snapped, and his gaze met hers again. She could dish his flirting right back at him, because if there was one thing that was never going to happen, it was them.

Sex was one thing. An accidental lapse in judgment was excusable. But it was over.

"You think the floral shop offers nothing? That's where you're wrong. There's more to Baughman Home Goods than just the warehouse."

"Nothing profitable. Which is why they're separate."

That made her seethe. She'd show this smug man a thing or two, starting with restoring the flower department to its role as a major player in the business.

"I disagree."

Jake ran his free hand over his neck. "There's nothing there. It's our office now and has literally brought in zero money for the last several years. Zero flowers. Zero."

"I know how to count to zero," she said in a sharp tone. "But you have to spend money to make money, and the flower shop will bring profit once it gets going in the right direction."

"I hate to break it to you, but you really are living in fantasyland."

"My fantasies are all grounded and obtainable, I assure you," she said, defending her genius idea that she wasn't going to waste her breath telling him about.

He just rested his wrist on the door frame and leaned in close enough so she could smell the fabric softener from his bedsheets faintly wafting from his warm skin. The man smelled like a Saturday morning she could get wrapped around.

"All of my fantasies are grounded and obtainable, too." He openly looked her from lips to eyes and smiled. "It's only a matter of time."

"And hard work," she stuttered, though she had a feeling they weren't talking about the same thing anymore.

"Oh, I'm willing to put in the work for the reward," he said, and that time his gaze paused extra long on her mouth, and yep, she knew they weren't talking about the business anymore.

"Again, I don't even like you," she said.

"Is that why you jammed your tongue down my throat last night?"

"That has nothing to do with liking you."

"All right. Then can you not like me all over again? I promise I'll not like you right back. Hard and slow and—"

"Is there a reason you sound so smug?" she asked. Hating that she had, but Jacob tended to bring out her sassy side, which normally she had no problem hiding. Until she'd accidentally had sex with him against his truck last night. Whoops. Now she had to be on high alert about everything she said, every move she made. Because both would be aimed at him if she wasn't careful.

"I just thought it was fair to talk about my fantasies since we talked about yours," he teased and stretched on purpose, running a palm over his hard stomach. "Just feeling good this morning. Had a good night, after all."

"Really? Because from my point of view it was a big problem."

"Two things." He held up his hands and counted them off. "One, I'm glad you noticed I'm big." He winked, and she rolled her eyes. "Second, I'm a problem solver, Miss Baughman."

That made her blush, and she instantly thought of last night. Yes, they'd had sex, but if his mind was anything like hers, all she thought about was reliving that moment. She'd even considered touching herself to ease the ache of withdrawal from him. Had he made himself come last night? Thinking of her? Why did the just the idea make her hot and—

"Jake?" a female voice called from inside.

Laura's eyes shot wide. He had a woman over? This early in the morning? He was half-naked and . . .

Oh hell no.

"Be right there," he called casually over his shoulder.

Fire raced through her veins. Had he seriously had sex with her last night and then still found time to get another woman to his house? She was learning quickly that Jake did mean what he said. And clearly, he'd taken another woman home last night. He had clearly changed so much since she'd known him ten years ago. How could she be so naive?

"Problem solver indeed," she said between gritted teeth and turned on her heel to walk away.

"Whoa, hold up," he said, coming after her and shutting the front door. Clearly he didn't want the woman inside hearing or seeing Laura. "Want me to give you a ride to work? Or at least back to your car you left at the bar last night?"

"No." She was not going near that truck again. Or him. "Enjoy your morning." She glanced over his shoulder to his house, where she saw a beautiful, dark-haired woman walk by the window. Like she knew where she was going. Like she was comfortable there. "And you're right. You certainly are a problem solver."

A wide grin broke over Jake's face, and she wanted to smack it right off him. He glanced behind him, then back at her, realizing she could see the woman through the windows.

"Hold up," he said with a small chuckle. Which did amazing things to those cut abs of his. "Are you jealous?"

"No!" she shot out quickly. "I just have work to do, and clearly you have something to do as well, so I'll be on my way."

"Oh yeah," he said. "You're jealous."

She huffed and got in his face. "Understand one thing right now, Jacob Lock. I'm a lot of things. Including resourceful, driven—"

"Stubborn," he said.

"Smart," she continued.

"Sexy."

She shook her head. "My point is, *jealous* is not one of them."

"Oh, I think you are."

"Well, perhaps you should keep one thing in mind when you're doing all that thinking." She took a step closer until her breasts touched his bare chest. She was going for intimidating but had to stifle a gasp at the contact and stay focused. "I am a Baughman and my name is on the business. Literally. And I'm going to make this shop work. With or without your help." She gave a hard glare to drive her point home. "So keep that in mind."

He smiled and leaned in. Just when she thought he might try to kiss her, he brought his coffee cup between them and took a sip.

"Yes, ma'am."

She nodded once and turned to walk off. The morning was cool and thankfully it wasn't raining and she needed to clear her head. Especially when Jacob called after her.

"Have a good day, *Miss Baughman*."

Chapter Five

Laura was rethinking her outfit choice about an hour into scrubbing out the coolers. So much for looking professional. She was on her hands and knees getting God knew how many years of filth out of the flower coolers. Good news was there was plenty of space for various flowers and arrangements. Just a little tidying up was all it'd take to get the shop looking niceish. And not like an office.

Okay, so it was a bit dated. Sure, you walked in and saw the old couch in the seating area and drab decor and it gave the vibe of 1987, but she could work with that. Mostly because she had to stay positive. With some fresh arrangements and the coolers and cases full of colorful options, it would set off the front desk and simple seating area.

She hoped.

She glanced over her shoulder to said seating area and calculated new chairs and an area rug into the mental budget she had in her mind.

She kicked off her heels and finished scrubbing the last cooler.

Next task was tackling the desk, which held dust—sawdust, more specifically—a computer from the nineties, and an even older printer.

Mentally calculating a laptop and Bluetooth printer . . .

Which would help the warehouse, too, so Jake could suck it. She glanced around, and anger flared at Jacob. Partly because she was *still* thinking of him naked, and the fact that she hadn't actually seen him *fully* naked—not that she cared. But she was more upset that he'd let this place go. He only cared about the dumb warehouse of mannish supplies in the back. But flowers were a part of this place, the legacy of her mother, and she'd be damned if they were left by the wayside.

The little bell over the front door dinged, and Laura turned to see the door swing open and Hannah walk through.

"Hannah?" Laura said, standing and dusting off her hands.

"I just wanted to come check this place out. You took off in a hurry last night."

Laura took a deep breath. "Yeah, just needed some fresh air."

"Uh-huh. And did you find it in Gabe's or Jake's mouth?"

"What?"

"Oh, come on, it was obvious both of them are after you."

She couldn't lie to her best friend. "I gave Gabe my number just as a friendly catch-up, considerate thing."

Which he'd taken seriously, since he'd already texted a few times and they'd made dinner plans to catch up later this week. Which Laura had agreed to—a friendly hangout. Not a date.

"So you got it bad for Jake, then?"

"No, I don't have anything for anyone. And if you were going to guess, smart money would be on the guy I gave my number to."

"Yeah, but you never go for the smart bet when it comes to guys," Hannah said.

She had a point there.

"Well, as fun as it would be to chat about my bad taste in men, how about we talk about something else?"

Hannah smiled. "Oh, come on, you have great taste in bad men. But this place looks amazing."

Laura dusted off her hands. Anything to get past her no-dating policy and change the subject.

"I'm hoping to really be up and running in a few days," Laura said. "I just need to finish cleaning and—"

"Obtain some flowers?" Hannah finished, glancing at the empty coolers. Laura's chest stuttered on a breath, because the simplicity of her problem was also overwhelming.

"Yeah, that's a top priority."

"How top of a priority?" Hannah asked, coming more inside. "Because you know that lame-ass thing I was telling you about? It's my boss's brother's reception, or party, or some shit." Hannah waved her hand like she was swatting an annoying fly away. "Anyway, he's throwing it at the bar, and apparently because I have tits he thinks I know how to decorate for a party. The one thing he wanted, though, was centerpieces for all the tables."

"Really?" Laura exclaimed. Then she tried to tamp down her excitement. Her best friend was also going to be her first customer. "I can do centerpieces. I just need an idea of what you like, how many, and your budget."

"I don't like flowers, so it's whatever you think, and I need twelve. The budget is a grand."

Laura nodded happily. She could pull that off. Flowers at wholesale couldn't be that expensive. Pair them with some cute vases and boom! She had a customer. She'd stand to make a profit if the centerpieces came in under seventy dollars apiece. Which they should. At least, she thought so . . .

"That's great. I can do that. When do you need these?"

"Is one week too soon?"

"Nope," Laura said quickly. "I can make that work." She'd make anything work if it meant getting a profit for the shop.

"You're a lifesaver," Hannah said, and for the first time, Laura felt good about herself. She was making progress—she had a customer and couldn't wait to shove this in Jacob's smug face. Flowers could be lucrative. Sure, it was her best friend needing flowers for a bar, but still. It counted as business. And she hadn't spent a dime. Which meant she could use some of the business money to get some start-up items and flowers, because she'd make it back. Perfect!

She just had to figure out how to get Jake to loan her some of that business money, since he was the stingy man in charge of the accounts.

"I have to get running to work, but come in and see me."

"Um . . . I'll try. I just have a thing later this week."

"A thing?" Hannah asked.

"It's not a date, but I told Gabe I'd have dinner and catch up with him."

"Oh, sure. And I bet he's real excited to catch you up with the party in his pants."

"Shut up," Laura said with a laugh.

"See you later, Queenie."

Hannah nodded and let herself out. Laura wanted to high-five herself. But she couldn't waste any time. Her dad used to keep his wholesale suppliers in a Rolodex around here somewhere . . .

She started looking through the office area. Opening drawers, which—surprise, surprise—had more sawdust in them. After a bit of hunting, she finally found the dusty spinner of contacts and started going through them.

She found the main supplier and the backup supplier, picked up the office phone, and dialed.

"Hello, this is Laura Baughman at Baughman Home Goods and I'd like to discuss a shipment of flowers for a rush delivery."

"Ah, Baughman? Like Walt?" the voice asked over the line.

"Yes, he's my father."

"Oh, well, I'm sorry, ma'am, but we've been out of the flower business for a few years now. The wife got into landscape design with my oldest. Is Jake needing to speak with me?"

Laura frowned. "I'm sorry, Jacob Lock? Why would he speak with you?"

"Well, he runs Baughman Home Goods and is set to deliver the thick chip bark I ordered next week. Is everything all right? We're still on for the order, right? Because I need that bark."

Laura's mouth hung open, and she frowned and shook her head. "I . . . yes, I suppose it's fine. I mean, I assume he's still going to deliver your bark."

"Assume? Is that why you're calling me?"

"I'm calling because I thought you supplied flowers at wholesale."

"That was years ago. *You* supply me with bark. Is Jake there? Maybe I should talk to him. This is—"

"No," Laura said quickly. "He's not here. I'm sorry for the confusion. Have a good day."

The man mumbled something, and Laura hung up fast. How had this happened? The flower wholesaler now was using Baughman for their orders? Through Jake? Holy hell, the world was backward. She was ready to throw the phone across the room. Or maybe herself. The man who'd once supplied Baughman was now being supplied by Baughman? And now she looked like the idiot.

Frickin' great . . .

She dialed the secondary wholesaler, determined to be stealthier this time and feel out the situation. But she got a disconnected number. After a few Google searches on her phone, she realized that they were also out of business.

Which meant that she had her first customer . . . and no flowers.

"Tough day at the office?" Jake called from his relaxed seat on the porch of his house as he watched Laura strut her perfect ass up his driveway.

It was a bright summer evening on the coast. Not a cloud in the sky. And Laura's skin looked extra tan with every ray that hit her legs. The woman was meant for the sunshine.

"It's a flower shop that just so happens to have an office. Not *the* office, and it was a good day, thank you very much."

He nodded and took a swig of beer. "I can see that."

The woman was covered in dust and her pretty outfit was wrinkled, as if she'd been doing a whole lot of moving and bending. Something he'd love to have seen. But the outfit didn't match the scenery. Laura may have been raised here once upon a time, but she was a high-class city girl. One who looked like she'd just had a taste of manual labor.

He was both impressed and turned on, because the prom queen was hot when she was pristine, but a little dirty? She was sexy as hell. And he had the need to show her what kind of dirty he was willing to make her.

"In fact," she said with a snap of happiness in her voice, "today was extra great, because I've acquired my first customer."

Jake could hear the pride in her voice. He still couldn't help poking at her, though, because the truth remained that the flower shop contributed jack shit to the business as a whole. Sure, he was happy she was happy. Wait, he should be upset about that. Or at the very least he shouldn't care. But her smile was wide even though her face held signs of a long day, and the first thing he felt the need to do was pull her closer and ask questions. Maybe tuck that lock of stray hair behind her ear while she told him about her day.

He closed his eyes briefly. It was that kind of thinking that he needed to be careful of. Between the business and her camping in his front yard, he couldn't really avoid her. And yet, it was too much . . . but not enough.

He wanted to know more. To hear her voice. Purely from professional curiosity about the business, of course . . .

"That's great you got a customer," he started. "But you have nothing to sell them."

She walked even closer, right up to his porch, but didn't step on it. Her glare hit him hard, and he smiled around a swig of his beer.

Damn, he loved her feisty side. Crazy how a woman could be so passionate . . . when she showed up, that was.

"Oh, I have something to sell. Actually, it's a *multiple flower order* for a party, and it's going to be great."

He nodded. He didn't doubt she was capable. But she needed to see for herself the hole she was digging. If she wanted to spin her wheels and spend her money on this grand idea, fine. It would be a hard lesson learned, but maybe then she'd see that the floral part of the business wasn't worth hanging on to.

"Well, good for you," he said and tipped his beer toward her in a salute.

She put a hand on her hip and blew a lock of hair of her eye. The same one he'd just been thinking about. She looked him over as if not impressed, but the slight flush in her cheeks when her gaze hit his chest told him she was a little impressed.

"Enjoying your day off, I see."

"Yep." He took another hearty swallow of beer. "It's been a while since I've had a weekend off. And when something good comes along, I take full advantage."

"I'm sure you do," she muttered.

Jake saw her peek around at the large, open windows into his house.

"Still jealous about the woman who was here earlier? She's gone, you know."

Laura shrugged. "I don't care about that in the least. Actually, I was just noticing how you have a pretty pathetic setup in there."

"Well, don't spare me the truth of how you really feel."

But her words made Jake look over his shoulder into his house. His leather sofa and big-screen TV were noticeable. Hardwood floors. It was nice. So he had bare walls and no real sense of a cozy vibe, pictures, art, whatever. And yeah, in the daylight it did look a bit sterile. But he didn't need any of that. He really didn't. But Laura was real close to becoming the second woman of the day to criticize his house.

But for some reason, Laura bringing it up bugged him more than his sister. Like . . . he wanted to impress her or something.

"What's wrong with my place?" he asked.

"It's empty," she said. "It's just . . . depressing, really."

"Coming from a woman who lives in that." He pointed at the fifth wheel. "People who live in campers shouldn't throw stones at gorgeous, custom-built homes."

"At least it's lived-in and warm."

Jake wanted to argue, but honestly, he didn't have much, because his ex had taken most everything, and whatever she hadn't taken, he'd gotten rid of. He didn't want reminders of her or the life he'd planned to have. It was just him now. In a house. Alone.

Sparse.

Yep, that about summed it up.

"I like it how it is," he said and barely sounded convincing. "And besides, using words like *warm* doesn't mean the camper is nice. That's code for cluttered and messy."

Her brow peaked. "Really? That's what you think? Well, then . . ." She turned and walked toward the camper. "Why don't you come see for yourself?"

Jake was off his seat and on her heels in record time. "I was wondering when you were going to invite me in," he said against her ear as he stood behind her while she unlocked the door.

She spared him a glace over her shoulder. "I'm not inviting you in. You can look, but you can't touch. And only so I can prove you wrong."

Sounded like Jake's situation at the moment with the sultry blonde. Look but don't touch, and always the competition.

"Okay," he acknowledged. "Then how about after the grand tour I take you to dinner?"

What the hell was he doing? Nothing smart. But after a day alone in an empty house, he wanted to talk to Laura more. Get caught up in her wide eyes and happy ideas. Hear her voice go up and down in volume with excitement.

"No dating," she said drily.

"You have to eat sometime," he said. For now. Because he wanted another night with Laura. "I'm ready to be wowed."

She smiled and opened the door. She walked through, and Jake placed both his hands on the door frame and leaned in to get a good look.

"Holy hell," he said in surprise. The place was clean, smelled like vanilla and fresh rain, and was . . . warm. He kept his spot on the outer step but shoved his big body through the doorway a bit more to look around. There were pops of color everywhere. A little vase of flowers on the small, two-person table. The bed was made up with a purple, gold, and cream quilt and matching pillowcases. He blinked to clear away the mirage he was seeing. Because this had to be a mirage.

Laura sat at the table and reached down to take off one heel, then the other.

"I love that face," she said, looking at him with pure joy.

Jake frowned. "What face?"

"The one you're making now," she said. "You're impressed and realize that I'm right. It's nice in here. May not be a . . . what was it? Gorgeous, custom-built house? But it's homey. And it's mine."

Jake glanced around again. She was right. It was homey. So much that he wanted to come inside. Have a cup of coffee with her. Because every inch of the camper was all her. And Walt. It was a Baughman place. And damn if he didn't desperately want to be a part of that.

"You can let yourself out now," she said.

Jake nodded once. They were right back to square one. Which really sucked, because he was trying for more squares. But he was growing increasingly confused. She'd obviously spent hours cleaning this place. Between that and making that list of hers, she must not have slept at all last night. But she'd made the camper her own. Would that make her stick around this time and not take off at the next best opportunity? He didn't get how someone like Laura could be so wrong, yet so right.

Wrong for him, at least. He'd been burned once and knew better than to trust her kind of woman. The kind that was constantly eyeing the bigger, better deal. But there was a kindness to her. A good work ethic. A spirit of ambition.

Yes, he liked her.

Had for a long time.

But he still had to be smart. Responsible. Sort of.

Nothing about her made sense, and he was starting to feel like a key puzzle piece was missing.

"I really do like what you've done with the place," Jake said honestly. "And the woman today at my house was my sister."

She paused and looked up at him. Jake figured Laura hadn't gotten a good look at her and even if she had, Erica had changed a lot in the past decade. A flash of emotion spread over Laura's face. Sadness, happiness, relief? It was so complex he couldn't pinpoint it. But there was a slight downturn of her mouth that made him think she was hurting.

He didn't know why he'd said that, but he'd felt like he had to. To clear the air. To let her know he wasn't with anyone but her.

"It's your life," she said. "I'm not asking questions."

With one last look at her, he stepped down. He was officially on the outside and she was on the inside. And for some reason, his big, beautiful, custom-made house didn't feel so great at the moment.

She wasn't asking him questions. Wasn't asking him in. In fact, he stood there, with the sun starting to set, wishing he could do some of the asking. First question would be why she had a sad look in her eyes. Why she was working so hard at something that was doomed. Why was she so . . . relentless?

Wanting to know Laura Baughman was a bad thing. He should be concentrating on keeping his distance, not wondering what she was doing later and if she'd ever consider having dinner with him.

He tried again.

"Laura," he said despite his better judgment. "I'd like to take you to dinner. Any night, you pick."

Her eyes looked soft; then she said, "I can't. I have plans."

"All week?"

She nodded. "I can't do dinner with you, Jake."

That's when the events of last night hit him. "Can you do dinner with someone else? Like Deputy Quarterback?"

She didn't say anything. And the longer Jake stood there, the more he felt like an outsider. Literally.

"Enjoy your night," he said. And the child in him wanted to hope she didn't.

Chapter Six

Laura needed to talk to her dad. This business with Jake was getting . . . complicated. It had been three days since the truck incident. And by incident she meant crazy, amazing sex. But it was a new week, and she had gone as far as she could with the shop on zero dollars.

She needed some investment money, and since Baughman was a business, which included both the warehouse and the shop, she was hoping her father would see reason and let her use some of the company money to buy flowers.

She already had a slam dunk with this order from Hannah.

The sun was just starting to set over the ocean as she walked down Main Street, toward Bubba's Subs, where her father had told her to meet him.

Only when she came to the sandwich shop, she realized quickly that Bubba's Subs was no longer in business. Rather, it was now Berta's Britches and Brassieres.

"Oh no. No, no, no," Laura muttered to herself as she stared down the front window display of lingerie. A mannequin wearing a sequined bra with cups sewn to look like beach balls was waving at her.

This was an ambush.

Laura turned to walk—run—away, but the jingle bell of the door opened and a familiar voice rang out.

"Laura! Get your skinny behind in here. Your daddy said you were coming by!"

Laura turned to find Roberta in a black leather tank top, arms wide-open in greeting, standing in the doorway.

"Berta's lingerie. Of course," Laura said, slowly walking into the giant bosomy hug that was waiting for her.

"And you're just in time," Roberta said, switching over the CLOSED sign in the window and tugging Laura inside. "My Lusty Ladies book club is here, and as promised, there's plenty of Chex Mix and Merlot for one more lusty lady." Roberta winked and gave Laura a side hug as she ushered her through the store and toward the back.

The sounds of chatty women came from the back room while Laura couldn't help but take in the amazing store. Beautiful displays of intricately sewn lingerie were proudly displayed, and Laura caught herself staring at a red lace number hanging on the far wall. The place was bright with colors, but the room was soft and glowing, as if lit by candlelight. Just really good dimming, it seemed. Everything was classy and lovely and unique. That's when it hit Laura: Roberta loved color and had a shop full of creative fabrics, just like Laura's mother had loved color and had a shop full of creative flowers.

Maybe Roberta was better for her dad than she'd realized.

"You like it?" Roberta asked as they swayed past a rack of garter belts, the soft clicking of the clasps ringing through the air as they shrugged past them.

"Roberta, this is really an incredible shop," Laura admitted.

But as they came to the back and Laura saw three ladies sitting around a small wood table littered with copies of *Cowboy Kink* and—yep—a bowl of Chex Mix, Laura had a flare of nerves.

"My dad said to meet him here?" she asked.

Roberta laughed. "Oh, honey, your daddy never comes to my ladies' night. Besides, he's avoiding you."

"What?" Laura said in surprise. "But he said—"

"Yeah, I know, but he wants you and Jake to work out your issues these next few weeks. Besides, this gives you and me a chance to hang out."

He could have just said that. But then again, Laura wouldn't have shown up. Cunning old man. She just needed a plan B, because she was running out of time and options and didn't want to go to Jake for money for the business. One, because he wouldn't give it to her, and two, the man was stubborn and she hated the idea of asking for something that should be part of the business already. Not because she was trying to be a brat, but because she really did want to do this on her own. Not with Jake holding her shop in his hands. His strong, rough, incredible hands.

No way was she asking him for money. It was bad enough she was already considering going to him for another orgasm or two. But she had to get flowers for Hannah's order.

"Roberta, I really need to speak with my dad."

"Sorry, honey. He's out looking at the plans for one of those custom log cabins."

"What?"

Roberta nodded and handed her a copy of *Cowboy Kink* and pulled out a chair. "Cal James is building this subdivision of sorts on the outskirts of town, only all the homes are supposed to look like log cabins. We're looking into buying one."

Laura's brows shot up. Not just because she knew of Cal James. She'd gone to high school with him, and though they'd never hung out, she'd thought he was one of those genius types in the AV club. She was more shocked that her father really was moving on. Buying a house with Roberta and all.

"This is Tilly, Cynthia, and Esther," Roberta said, introducing the Lusty Ladies.

"Here, kiddo, you'll need this for the topics we're covering tonight. Don't worry, Cynthia will catch you up on everything," Tilly said, handing Laura a big glass of wine and pointing to the book.

"It really is so nice to meet you," Laura started, because she couldn't stay. Not here, not with these women who were looking at her like they'd just found a stray kitten. "I really do have a ton to get done and figure out—"

"Oh, honey, you want to get ahead around here, we're your best bet. Now sit your cute behind down and get comfy," Roberta said, gently shoving on Laura's shoulder so she plopped in her seat. Her wine swished, and Roberta took a seat next to her.

Laura blew out a breath. She'd have to thank her father later for this setup. Not only was he avoiding her, but he'd sicced his lady friend on her to be . . . friends?

Laura didn't even know how to start to handle this.

"You know, Travis McCreedy is starting up a ranch," Tilly said, tapping her copy of *Cowboy Kink*. "He's the hero in this book. He has problems, too. Kind of like your flower shop. Only he needs cows and there's a land dispute."

"Of course, that's when Georgia comes in and helps him out . . ." Cynthia said with a giggle.

"Yeah, helps him out of his belt buckle. That barn scene with those two going at it in the hay was hot!" Tilly cut back in.

Oh God, this was happening. Laura sat there and just chugged down her wine while her father's girlfriend and her friends chatted about a book and sex in a barn. She'd need a few more glasses to calm the chaos rising in her stomach.

She needed support and flowers, and what she'd gotten was zero answers, an avoidant father, and sex talk she was trying to stay away from, because sex or talk of any kind only made her think of Jake.

"You know, Travis will get that big deal he needs. Just like you, Laura," Roberta said.

"Pardon?" Laura asked. Was she really comparing a dirty-book cowboy to her situation?

But Roberta simply nodded. "You starting the flower shop. You need a big deal to land some profit and get that sexy foreman off your tail, right?"

"Ah, yeah," Laura replied. Roberta seemed to be more in the loop than she'd realized.

"Well, there you are, just like Travis." She tapped the book. "You just need to find your big break. Like a large land development project looking for plants and flowers for a local subdivision . . . for example."

Laura's eyes shot up. She'd gone to school with Cal and was pretty sure he was smart back then, but heading up a major building project like this, the guy was clearly doing well for himself. But was Roberta really giving her a hint as to what to go for?

"Cal is looking for a supplier and landscape designer?" Laura asked.

Roberta smiled. "That's the word on the street. He mentioned wanting someone savvy in marketing, too."

Laura looked around. Maybe these Lusty Ladies weren't so bad after all. And she could use some insider info—not to mention friends.

"That would be a great opportunity," Laura admitted. Then she scoffed and took an angry sip of her wine. "But I can't even get funding from the business to fulfill a small flower order, much less the money to set up a mock proposal for a big deal like Cal's subdivision."

Roberta frowned. "Just go to the bank and take out some money. What's hard about that?"

"I can't. It's all under Baughman Home Goods."

"Right, which your name is on."

Laura choked on her sip of wine. "What's that?"

Roberta just smiled again. "Your dad has your name and Jake's on there, of course. It's always been on all the accounts, honey. And the insurance. He knew you'd come back one day."

Laura wanted to hug Roberta. Her father might be avoiding her, but his lady friend appeared to be happy to help. And this new information turned everything around for Laura, the shop, and the future.

"You know what," Laura said, finishing her wine, "I'm going to need some Chex Mix and someone to catch me up on this barn scene."

She settled into her chair and the women hooted.

It appeared that Laura was the newest member of the Lusty Ladies, and the first order of business was to exercise exactly what that title meant.

Chapter Seven

"I'm so screwed, Hannah," Laura said, staring at outfit option number 1,453 she'd tried on tonight. It had been a tough few days, but she'd done what Roberta had said and gone to the bank and made a small withdrawal from the Baughman Home Goods account. Problem was, she still couldn't find anyone local, or even close to local, to buy her flowers wholesale from. And Hannah's order was due soon.

"I thought the point was to dress so that you can literally get screwed . . . in that case, I'd go for the last dress with more cleavage," Hannah said.

Hannah sat on her bed blowing bubbles with her gum and giving her a world-class critique while Laura tried on Hannah's entire closet. Just like they'd done a thousand times back in the day.

"I'm not trying to screw Gabe. And this isn't a date. I need something modest. And all of your clothes are . . ."

Laura tugged on the low-cut neckline of Hannah's green dress.

"Slutty?"

"No!" Laura said. "You just have a different style than I do."

"Yeah, no shit. You dress business casual for Friday night at the local bar."

"Which is why I'm here raiding your closet, thank you very much."

Hannah nodded and came up behind Laura and looked in the mirror over her shoulder. "You look hot. You just need to do whatever feels comfortable."

Laura tugged on the dress to try to cover a bit more leg. The bodice was tight, but the skirt flared just enough to give a casual summer feel. Paired with a denim jacket, it was cute for a simple nondate. But it was just a bit short. Laura tugged on the hem again.

"Seriously?" Hannah said. "I'm five three and you're seven three. All my dresses are going to be short on you."

Laura rolled her eyes. "Thanks a lot."

"Well, it would help if you quit trying to dress for the wrong guy."

"I'm not dating Jake. I'm going to dinner with Gabe, which isn't a date, either," Laura replied quickly.

"I was talking about Gabe. He's the wrong guy."

Laura spun and frowned. "No, Jake is the wrong guy. Gabe is great—"

"On paper. Fits you like a perfect cliché in a Sandra Bullock movie. He's the quarterback, you're the prom queen, and the two of you can run off into the sunset and have two point four kids and a white picket fence."

"And that's the wrong guy?" Laura asked.

"Yeah, because you would have taken that option by now if he wasn't."

Hannah had a point. She could have dated Gabe in high school. Taken his letterman jacket and class ring and gone down the simple, steady path that was outlined for her. But she hadn't been interested then. Because she'd wanted out. Wanted an adventure. Wanted to escape. She hadn't wanted to deal with her mother's death or even acknowledge her own mortality. Which was why she'd made the decisions she had. The wrong decisions.

"Instead I wasted my twenties on an asshole and wound up a divorcée at nearly thirty and living in my dad's camper."

"Hey, at least you go for what you want. You're ambitious. That's what I love most about you. Sure, you've made some bad picks, but who hasn't? The NFL draft has you beat by far in picking the wrong guys."

She smiled at her friend. Hannah had a way of making her feel better, and yet, Laura still felt like she wasn't quite there. She was trying. But no answers seemed clear.

"Well, the men don't matter. What does is flowers," Laura said.

"Wait, we're going to talk about the shop now and you're not going to tell me all the juicy details on how you got screwed against a truck by a hot guy?"

"I'm really regretting telling you even that little detail," Laura mumbled.

"So it's little, huh?"

"No, he's huge!" Laura slapped a palm over her mouth, and Hannah laughed.

She may have called her friend the other night to tell her about the outdoor sexy time in the middle of a deserted road with Jacob Lock against his Chevy. And now she was getting that little fact thrown back in her face, and Hannah had a way of getting details.

"Oh, come on," Hannah said. "I'm proud of you for taking charge, not getting caught up, and just doing what you need to do. And if one of those things you need to do is a sexy local, then I'm in full support of you."

Laura smiled. "I'm not dating anyone, and I need to get through dinner tonight with Gabe as friends."

"Why did you agree to see him, anyway?"

"Because I want to live here, and being friends with the deputy is a good start. I'm going to see him around and can't avoid him. Might as well establish boundaries now—that way we can have a cordial, nice friendship."

"Sounds hot," Hannah said with sarcasm. "Guys love nothing more than boundaries and cordiality."

Laura shook her head and reexamined the green dress. Maybe it wasn't so bad? It did show a little more leg than she usually went for.

And the V cut showed subtle cleavage. She got a surge of heat thinking of Jake. Would he like the dress?

He's not the one you're seeing tonight, moron.

Right! She wasn't seeing anyone, per se. She was focused. On the shop.

"But seriously," Hannah said. "It sounds like you've had a productive week. Between getting the flower shop going and outside truck sex, you're really taking life by the balls here in small-town Oregon."

"I'm trying," she said. "But I'm hitting a snag in my grand plan."

She wanted to build a life, a home here. She wanted a lot of things. But first was stepping out on her own and really thriving. Connecting to her mother, her town, was something she was clinging to.

"I have real problems here," Laura said, trying to get back on topic. "I need flowers for your order and I can't find a wholesaler. Seriously, how sad is that? I run a flower shop with no flowers."

"It'll be okay," her friend said. *Yeah, easy for her to say.* Laura had spent the last twenty-four hours trying to hunt down a wholesaler she could build a rapport with, and she hadn't even found one she could get a single order from.

"Maybe order online? You'll pay extra for shipping, but maybe some wholesalers will overnight to you. If you're thinking big, then you have to act big. Can't go with the localish wholesalers."

Laura had thought of that. "It's just more expensive, because I'd have to order in bulk. And a lot. Which means more money up front."

But she might not have a choice.

"Well, if you have extra on hand, you could use it to set up a sample. Try for new business."

"Yes, that's true," Laura agreed. "There is a big job I heard about that I'm trying to go for."

"Yeah? Tell me about it."

Laura felt a little unsure since it was just town gossip. "Cal James is hiring a landscape designer for the subdivision. I was thinking I could supply the plants and flowers, and that kind of contract would get the flower shop back on the map."

"Then you should go for it!" Hannah said.

She could use a bit more money up front to cover the costs. Just borrowing from the business account. She'd put it back, and her dad had said she and Jake had to work it out. Thanks to Roberta's inside bit of knowledge, she knew Jake didn't own the account—Laura's name was on it, too. This was a smart business decision. At least if she had to order more, she'd have extra on hand for walk-in customers. She just hoped they'd like the flowers she picked . . .

"I think I'll have to go that direction."

Hannah nodded. "With the flowers or the dress?"

Laura looked herself over in the mirror one more time. "Both."

Maybe the green dress was a mistake. Or maybe it was perfect. Laura didn't know how she felt about it since she'd been at Goonies only a few minutes and Gabe had glanced at her breasts three times already. Granted, he was trying to be a gentleman. But still. This wasn't a date.

"I'd be happy to take you to Benetti's," Gabe said for the second time in five minutes. It was the nice Italian restaurant on the edge of town, but Laura didn't want a date, and it was clear that's what Gabe was going for. So Goonies it was.

"With it being such a beautiful day, I thought hanging out here, maybe outside, would be nice," Laura said. She left out *casual*. Because that's what this was. It was early evening and the sun was shining and hot, and Goonies had a great patio area complete with lawn games and oversize Jenga.

Yep, just two friends hanging out. Which Gabe didn't seem crazy about.

But Laura grabbed her beer and Gabe grabbed his, and she made for the patio.

"We could play corn hole?" Laura offered. Tossing beanbags at a square platform with a hole cut out seemed like a way to stay active . . . and keep Gabe on one end of the lawn and her on the other.

"Sure," Gabe said, less than amused.

"I'm glad we can hang out and be friends," Laura said, grabbing red beanbags and taking her place on one side of the lawn while Gabe went to the other. They each stood next to a platform to throw at.

"Yeah, friends hanging out," Gabe said, tossing a beanbag in his hand. "Just like old times."

"Gabe . . . ," she said and he just shrugged. "I want to be friends. I'm sorry, I'm not dating at all right now."

He nodded and then tossed out that smile he used on all the cheerleaders back in the day. "Hey, a guy can try. And I'll keep trying, Laura."

Wish you wouldn't . . .

Instead of yelling, "Never going to happen" to the deputy of Yachats, she took a swig of beer and geared up to make her first toss.

"You care to make this interesting?" a low voice whispered in her ear, and Laura jumped. She turned to see Jake. All six-plus feet of hulking sex on a stick of him. Wearing a tight white T-shirt and blue jeans, he looked as good as he smelled. Which was really, really good. Like sandalwood and man. But it had nothing to do with his coastal roots. This spicy scent was all him.

"What are you doing here?" Laura asked, trying to refocus on her impending toss. Gabe was four yards away, standing next to the platform she was aiming for, and judging by the look on his face, not thrilled she was talking to Jake.

Not that it was his right in the first place.

"I'm on a casual date. Just like you," Jake said.

"I'm not on a date, we're just friends hanging out."

"Uh-huh," Jake said just as his date walked up to join them. "Me, too."

"Vicky McPhee?" Laura asked as the skinny brunette came to stand by Jake and threaded a hand through his arm. As if making a display she was there with him. Yeah, Laura got the message.

"Laura, it's been a long time," Vicky said, giving her hair a toss.

Laura tried for her best polite smile, but it just came out fake. Vicky McPhee had been captain of the cheerleading team, and even though she and Laura had run in the same circle, she'd made her life hell. And judging by the way she was clinging to Jake, not much had changed.

"We were just discussing teams," Jake said.

No, we weren't.

"Why don't you be on my team," he said to Vicky. She giggled and swayed and agreed.

Barf.

"You run on down to stand next to Gabe." Jake waved to the deputy; then Vicky frowned, catching on that to be on a team you needed one person on each side.

"Fine, this way I get a better view," she said to Jake and winked at him.

Double barf.

She walked toward Gabe and took her spot beside him just as Jake inched closer to Laura and picked up the blue beanbags.

"You weren't even invited to this game," Laura said to Jake, thanking God that between the music and the distance, Vicky and Gabe were out of earshot.

"But you don't mind, do you?" Jake said with sarcasm. "Just a *friendly* competition with *friends.*"

He was overstating the word *friend* to irritate Laura, and it worked.

"Just like you and Vicky are *friends,*" she said, not looking at him, instead focusing on taking her first shot. It hit the board but slid off. No points.

"You look a little rusty with this game," Jake said close to her ear. "You have to set your stance. It's all in the legs," he said, and just then, she felt his fingertips slowly trail up the back of her thigh, not stopping until he reached the hem of her dress.

"Are you done groping me yet? This won't give you an edge. I plan on winning," Laura informed him.

"Oh, I know you do. But I thought I'd remind you how much you like my touch."

"That's absurd."

She tossed again. Barely missed!

"You're not moving my hand away," Jake said, calling her out.

Oh, right. That would be because she liked his touch. But he definitely couldn't know that. She couldn't go swatting at his hand, though; otherwise, Gabe and Vicky down there would see the action and it would be obvious that Jake and Laura were . . .

They were nothing.

Not dating.

Not anything.

But Jake was right. She wasn't moving his hand away. She huffed out a deep breath and squeezed her last beanbag just as Jake's fingers continued the trail up the back of her thigh and barely went beneath her skirt. Her stupid body responded to his stupid touch, and she hated that a flare of heat hit hard between her legs. She had to bite back a groan, because she wanted him. Bad.

But he was there with Vicky.

She was there with Gabe.

Dating or not, this was annoying. She glanced over her shoulder to see Jake staring at her with a challenging brow arched. He looked good. He knew it. Vicky knew it. Hell, everyone knew it. But while Laura might not be swatting his hand away, Jake clearly wasn't pulling back on his own accord, either.

She smiled sweetly at him then refocused on tossing the bag.

She could play this game, too. Literally.

She bent over slightly and heard Jake's breath hitch. That was when she harnessed all the confidence she had, tossed, and . . .

"Direct hit!" Gabe called from across the lawn as Laura sank the beanbag in the hole.

"Yes!" she said with victory and faced Jake. "You're up. Good luck hitting that."

Jake smiled. "I love it when your competitive side comes out," he said. He tossed a bag effortlessly, sinking his first shot. Laura's shoulders deflated. Of course he was a pro at this, too. "You forget, though, I've got a lot of practice and plan to hit this"—he tossed again; it sank again—"all night long."

Laura took a long drink of her beer. "You done yet?" Because she could read into the innuendo. But what bothered her the most was wondering if he was insinuating *all night* with her—or with Vicky.

"I'm just getting warm," Jake said and paused to look her up and down while palming the last beanbag. She might like his touch, but Jake clearly liked what he saw. Time to let that competitive side of hers really breathe.

She took off her jacket, letting Hannah's dress do what it did best—flatter the girls. Which Jake noticed. Laura took a deep, deep breath until the fabric stretched tight . . .

Was Jake drooling?

Good.

She slowly exhaled and took another drink of her beer, then pointed at the platform.

"You have one last shot there, ace," she said.

Jake shook his head, refocused, shot, and . . .

Missed.

Laura faked a pouty face. "Too bad you couldn't close the deal," she whispered in her own sense of victory.

She stepped back and out of eye contact with Jake, because her skin was buzzing already. She watched Gabe and Vicky take their turns from the other end of the field, and Laura couldn't help but wonder how much competition she could take before she'd need an outlet for the rising tension.

~

Laura was *not* pacing in her camper, stopping only to peek through the window to see if Jake was home yet. Nope. She was definitely not doing that.

Gabe had dropped her off twenty minutes ago, and after the debacle of a not-date double date of sorts with Jake and Vicky, Gabe hadn't even walked her to her door. Which had been fine. Safe to say that the boundaries were set and hopefully she and the deputy could really be just friends.

Speaking of just friends, Laura just wanted to forget Jake's touch and his voice, and how he looked so damn hot in a simple T-shirt. She also didn't want to think about how he was still probably at the bar with Vicky.

She peeked out her window again.

She shouldn't care. Jake could do whatever he wanted. He was a single man and could date. Especially since Laura had told him she'd never date him. A fact she was kind of regretting. Granted, she hadn't thought he'd go out with a she-demon like Vicky frickin' McPhee, but whatever. Still, Laura knew it was smart to keep her focus on the shop and her own growth.

The sound of big truck tires coming up the driveway made her perk up.

Jake.

In his truck.

Alone.

And she wasn't feeling very smart at the moment.

He parked and climbed out of his Chevy just as Laura threw open the camper door to stomp toward him.

"What the hell do you think you're doing?" she yelled, closing in on him.

He walked around his truck and faced her. "I'm coming home."

"I mean tonight. You touch me, tease me, then watch me leave with Gabe and you go to Vicky's or something as if I won't care? What do you think is happening here?"

He closed that last few steps between them and threaded his hand in her hair at her nape.

"I think I'm getting you to reconsider your no-dating policy with me."

He didn't let her respond or even fight that comment. He just kissed her. Hard. And Laura was so mad, so hot, that she shoved her tongue between his lips and took a deep draw of him.

He growled.

She bit his lip.

He growled louder.

"Vicky McPhee?" she said with disgust between angry kisses. "How cliché to take the head cheerleader out to make me jealous."

"Says the prom queen who showed up with the quarterback," he countered.

He tugged her hair and dived in for another punishing kiss.

"And I knew you were jealous," he said between nibbles on her lower lip.

"So were you."

"Damn straight I was," he gruffed. "I want you, Laura. I've never denied that."

He kissed down her neck. That amazing mouth sent tingles through her body and lit up her skin like the Fourth of July. She didn't know if it was the pent-up aggression or the way Jake bit her earlobe, but she breathed the one thing that was the honest truth.

"I want you, too, Jake. So much."

She hugged him close, and he picked her up. She instantly wrapped her legs around him. Her dress was rucked up around her waist, and she felt his jeans-clad cock press against her core. She really did need him. Now.

"I won't be second to Vicky McPhee," she said and kissed him hard.

"I dropped her off and said good night. I was anxious to get back to you," Jake admitted.

And Laura had been anxious for him to get back.

"Then prove it," she said with a smile. With one hand reaching between their bodies, she unfastened his belt. "Now."

"Yes, ma'am," he said.

She had no idea how Jake did it. He was either part magician or incredibly strong, because he balanced Laura in one arm while he managed to get his jeans down far enough for his cock to spring free, and covered himself in a condom.

He turned and put her back against the truck.

"Now?" he asked.

"Yes," she begged, clawing at his back and shifting her hips, trying to take his length inside her, but he just continued to slide along her wet folds, which only drove the heat—the need—higher.

Using his cock, he moved her panties aside and surged deep.

"Oh God! Jake!" she cried out as he withdrew and pounded back inside.

"All night, you in this dress . . . ," he said between breaths and thrusts. "This is what I was imagining." He fucked her hard, her ass banging against his truck, and Laura's grip tightened as her whole body tensed with the need for the release she'd been dying for all night. Because like Jake, she'd thought about it, too. A lot.

"Tell me," Jake said. "Tell me I'm the only one that gets to see you like this."

Laura barely registered that Jake needed his own confirmation that she'd sent Gabe packing tonight. If only he knew how uninterested she was in the deputy.

"You're the only one, Jake."

She felt his smile on his lips. With a quick swipe of his hand, he tugged down the front of her dress, exposing her breasts. Her nipples beaded hard with the cool summer air, but Jake's mouth was right there to suck her.

She whispered his name again as he pumped in and out of her body while sucking her breast. The pleasure was too much, and Laura had no choice but to thread her fingers in his hair and let the tingles of her orgasm climb up her spine.

"You like this, don't you, baby?"

"Yes," she said. "So much."

"Then prove it," he said, using her words from earlier on her. "Come for me."

With her nails digging into his scalp and her teeth clamping down on his neck, she did.

White-hot lights flickered along her skin and melted every ounce of blood surging through her veins. She shook and trembled and begged for more. For Jake.

"I love my name in your mouth," he said.

And she believed him, because she felt him swell even harder inside her. His big muscles tensed. With a heavy groan that sounded like her name, he exploded.

Even with the condom, she felt him come hard and deep, and the movement of his impressive cock just spurred her own release to continue.

She'd never been so crazy, so needed before.

There, again, against his truck with her clothes in disarray, she clung to Jake, trying to steady her breaths. Because if she wasn't careful, she just might develop a pattern for attacking the sexy foreman at any given moment.

"One of these days, I'll get you to a bed," he said around a deep breath against her neck.

And that was what she was afraid of. Because at this rate, there was no place she'd rather be than in Jacob Lock's bed.

Chapter Eight

Snap, snap, snap!

Jake put the last three nails in the new siding of his sister's house and set the nail gun down on the grass, wiping his forehead with the back of his hand.

"Are you really done?" Erica asked, walking out with a glass of water.

"Yep, your new siding is up and ready to go," he said.

"No, I mean are you done avoiding your house and the warehouse?"

"I'm not avoiding anything," Jake said. "I've gone on a ton of drops and orders. And I'm helping you now."

"Oh, please. You live to work. And dropping off gravel keeps you out of the warehouse and away from the flower shop. Which is where Laura is. And you've spent the last two days nailing God knows what on my house for no reason."

"This is premium siding that helps with the elements of sea air and rain. You're welcome," he said. Erica just raised a brow, once again seeing right through him.

"Just go talk to her," she said.

"I don't know what you're talking about," Jake said, grabbing the water and taking several drinks.

"You like Laura. Good! About damn time you liked something more than work."

"Even if I did"—he did—"she won't go out with me." And hooking up had been amazing. Hell, he had a lot of pent-up feelings for her. And seeing her with Gabe the other night, only to be the one that got to see her at home, love on her, had been incredible. But Laura was holding firm on no dating, and Jake just felt like he was getting closer and closer to a woman who was keeping one hand on the door.

"Maybe it's time you start going after what you want," Erica said.

"I go after what I want," Jake replied.

"No, you don't. You sit and wait. Let things happen or let them go. You just . . . wait."

Jake couldn't exactly argue with that. He wanted Laura but wasn't jumping in entirely. He was still trying to be responsible. Find some way to make everything work. But every moment he spent with her, feeling her, seeing the woman she was and all that spirit she had, he just wanted to be more a part of her world.

Responsible or not.

He'd heard she'd been working hard at the shop the past couple of days . . .

"Maybe it's time I drop in to the flower shop," he said, and he didn't wait for his sister to say "duh" before he was already in his truck.

"Holy shit," Jake muttered as he walked into the office, which today looked a hell of a lot more like a flower shop. The coolers were filled with flowers, the smell of roses and lilies was pungent, and . . . was that new furniture in the waiting room?

"Oh, welcome to Baughman Home Goods. How may I help you?" Laura said sweetly, walking from the back room into the lobby. She looked pressed, pretty, and powerful. Three things he liked on her.

He'd gone out of his way to give her space the last two days. But with the weekend approaching, he couldn't keep busy staying away much longer or take on odd jobs for his sister. He'd had no idea she'd been up to something on this bigger scale in the office—flower shop. Clearly the woman could get a lot done in a limited time.

He also liked that she seemed to have an affinity for those skirts. Even though it was usually overcast here, she was her own special brand of sunshine in a big-city outfit. And Jake had to do a double take every time she walked in front of him.

Today she wore a silky cream top that looked like it could be see-through if he squinted hard enough, paired with a black leather skirt that hugged her hips and hit her knees, so he was doing more of a triple take. All the way down to, yep, bright red high heels.

Man, he liked that red on her. And she seemed to have a thing for the color, too.

"You did all this?" Jake asked.

"I like to jump in and get things accomplished," she replied with a smile. "Perhaps you just don't understand how to move quickly."

Oh, she was baiting him now. And, okay, he was impressed. He had no idea how much this must have set her back. A few grand, at least. Because she hadn't once come to him to ask for money from the business. She was putting her money where her mouth was and looking like she was following through on staying. But he still liked their playful chats.

"I can be quick. Start and finish before you even know I was around."

"Yes, I'm aware," she said drily and glanced at his cock then gave him a challenging scoff. *Oh hell no.* She had not just gone *there.*

"Despite my skills at quickies," he said, knowing she was thinking the same thing, "I still leave everyone involved satisfied. Even though it's not my expertise."

"Oh no? Then what is your expertise, Jacob?"

"Thoroughness." He took a step closer, because his jeans were getting tighter and she was just standing there looking lush and sexy, and damn, he'd missed her smart mouth over the past couple of days. He also seemed to be missing his brain, but he didn't care at the moment.

This woman's confidence, tenacity, and strength were getting to him. She was also easily the most gorgeous woman he'd ever seen. She might not be willing to date him, but that wouldn't stop him from trying. And in the meantime, she was doing something with him. Not Gabe. Not anyone else. Just him. And that was something.

"Well, I suppose you better get back to the warehouse," she said.

Jake had other plans. Ones that involved the woman in front of him.

"I'm in no rush to get back just yet," he said, creeping closer. He was locked in a stare down with Miss Baughman, and she wasn't backing down, either. Just circling, keeping her eyes on him until her perfect ass bumped against the edge of the desk.

"You're all set up here," he said, crowding into her space until she had no choice but to lean back. He heard the squeak of her leather skirt pressing against the edge of the desk. "I'm impressed."

"I'm not looking to impress you," she said. Her words had a bite, but the small shudder in her voice was enough to make him grin.

"Intentional or not, you are impressive," he said and dropped his chin enough to look in her eyes. She was staring up at him. Those big doe eyes and thick lashes were making his chest tighten.

He needed a taste of her. To feel her. Whatever battle he'd been fighting against the prom queen, he was losing. And judging by the way her breaths were shortening and her body trembled, Miss Baughman was on the brink of losing herself, too. He just hoped to God it was to him.

Laura couldn't think past anything but Jacob's mouth, which was hovering right over hers. He thought she was impressive? As much as she told herself she didn't care . . . she did. Because he sounded genuine. Like he really was . . . proud.

And that made her stomach flutter. Made her want to reach out and beg him to say it again. And again. But that was the opposite of what she should do. Should feel.

Should . . .

She should be strong and walk away. But she was currently pressed between a desk and wall of man, and she wasn't going anywhere. And she had missed him. Missed the way he could take her body with his like he owned it. Made her feel alive and wanted and strong.

She . . . liked him. A lot.

But he was also a pain and stubborn and so responsible he could be the Yachats High hall monitor for the rest of his days.

"Tell me the truth," Jacob said, his big hands cupping her waist and slowly trailing down her hips to her thighs. "Have you thought of me?"

"Of course I have," she said, wishing her voice wasn't so raspy. "You irritate me regularly and I'm forced to see you every day."

He smiled, and that was her tipping point. With a day's worth of scruff lining his jaw and that megawatt smile, she couldn't resist him. Her chest tightened like she couldn't get enough air, and her core flooded with the need to feel him again. Like the night he'd taken her against his truck. Or after her not-date date with Gabe. Every time Jake ravaged her body, it was better than the last.

"Forced, huh? Well, I'm sure sorry that my presence is such a struggle for you," he whispered, those big hands of his going even lower until he found the hem of her skirt right above her knees. "Let me see if I can give you a more pleasant memory."

Without warning, he slid his hands beneath her skirt and shoved it up her thighs as he picked her up and sat her on the desk.

"What are you doing?" She fidgeted to hike down her skirt, which was now bunched around her waist, but Jacob just hit his knees and tugged her legs open.

"If you don't know, then you're going to find out real quick." He tossed her legs over his shoulders and yanked her toward him. His face was buried between her thighs, and he kissed the insides of them as he tugged hard on her panties, ripping them clean off.

His mouth was hot against her skin, and her hands instantly threaded through his hair, tugging him closer. Wanting him to touch her, taste her, where she needed most. But he was teasing her. Running the tip of his nose along her folds, softly blowing on the heated flesh. And driving her crazy.

Her eyes snapped wide, and she realized where she was. Which was spread out on the desk with a wicked sexy foreman between her thighs.

"Someone will see!" she said and tried to squirm again.

A husky chuckle came from Jacob, and he gently bit the inside her thigh. Effectively stopping her poor excuse to get away. Because she didn't want to get away. She wanted to stay. Right there. With him between her legs.

"No one comes in here," he said.

"Hey!" she snapped. "I have a customer now. And the shop is open. People can come in at any time."

"Well, if you're that worried about it . . ." He flicked his tongue against her clit. Hard and fast, but enough to make her see stars and moan. "Then I can stop. It's your call."

That made her glare at him. Because they still didn't see eye to eye on things. But she might as well enjoy what she could, because she was so worked up, not even a bucket of ice water could cure this kind of heat.

Only Jacob could.

She pulled his hair hard and scratched his back with the sharp point of her stiletto. "Don't you dare stop," she said.

She felt his teeth scratch along her skin. His big, brawny arm wrapped all the way around her waist, and he pulled her onto his waiting tongue.

"Oh God!" she cried out and clung to the top of his head. She was almost falling off the side of the desk, but Jacob held her tight. Gravity was weighing her down and forcing her to take his stiff tongue deep.

He hummed, and Laura thought she'd instantly come just from that.

She rocked her hips, fucking his tongue and clawing at his scalp, searching for the release that was on the brink of taking her over already.

But he backed off just enough to lick her entire sex and suck hard on her clit.

Now this was impressive. "Please, please, please more."

She was panting. Begging. Needing him. And the way his mouth worked her over, flicking and eating at her like she was made of caramel, had her skin buzzing.

"Say it again," he rasped.

"Please, Jacob," she said. "Please give me more."

He gripped her tighter and plunged his free hand between her legs, thrusting one finger deep while he battered the sensitive bundle of nerves with his masterful tongue.

"Yes!" Her entire body lit up like a Christmas tree. Bright white lights twinkling behind her eyes and pleasure so hot and intense, she could feel the color red. Her sheath spasmed uncontrollably. Milking his finger and wanting even more of him with every lash of her release.

She was twisted up and concentrating on breathing, because her chest was too busy heaving from the intensity of pleasure to take full inhales.

She barely registered Jacob kissing her thighs as he rose. She leaned back on the desk, scooting just enough to keep her balance, because Jacob was still standing between her thighs.

He grabbed a condom from his pocked, ripped it open, and had his belt unfastened and himself covered in record time.

"Still want more?" he asked, running the head of his cock along her drenched folds.

"Yes," she said. "I'm eager to see this thoroughness you boast about."

"Be careful what you wish for," he said and surged his hips forward, burying himself inside her in one long thrust. He was so powerful that she couldn't support herself anymore.

He withdrew and surged back even harder. Deeper.

She moaned his name and gave in to all his strength.

She lay back on the desk, knocking over the phone and papers and other random things. She didn't care.

"God, you're so sexy," he growled and with one hand flicked the few buttons on her shirt open and tugged her bra down, wedging it beneath her breasts.

The cold air hit her chest, and her nipples beaded harder. But Jacob's mouth was right there to bring the heat. He leaned over her and sucked one, then the other. Circling the entire peak of her breast before gently biting and sucking it again.

She spread her arms out and arched into his mouth. But right as she was going crazy for him, he pulled back and rose to stand tall again.

"Wait, where are you going?" she asked.

"I'm still right here," he said and stirred himself inside her. His hip bones knocking against her inner thighs and the feel of him hitting that sensitive spot inside made a second orgasm kick into gear.

"I'm just being thorough, after all. I see you like this . . ." He stirred and stirred. His big hands clamped around her waist, thumbs digging into her pelvis, and he moved her body with his. Staying so deep, she felt him everywhere. "You like deep and slow, don't you?"

She nodded, because words escaped her. She couldn't form any even if she wanted to. All she could do was throw her hips out, trying to take more, but Jacob held her tight. Moving her how he wanted to. Slow, steady, thorough. But he seemed to pick up on her need and the orgasm boiling in her veins. Her sheath tensed once . . . then again.

God, she was so close!

He hit her with a victorious smile. "I feel you just fine. I know you're close," he said, as if reading her mind.

He lifted her hips, causing her to arch even farther so that only her ass and her shoulders were on the desk. It was enough for him to hit that spot inside once more and send her into a slow, steady, consuming release that burned her up from the inside out.

"Jacob . . . oh my God. It feels so . . ."

"Different?" he said, like he knew what he was doing. Because he did. She could feel the confidence in every move he made. The first orgasm was with his mouth, raw and fast and wild. This was only with him inside her, and it was smooth and fluid and intense. She'd never felt anything like it. Never been taken like this before.

Long, heavy breaths and she was coming down from the pleasure, but Jacob didn't seem to be through with her.

"You're not done yet," he said with a wicked smile. His big hands were still gripping her hips, keeping her arched and open to him. "If you don't want people to come in here, I suggest you prepare yourself to tamp down your screams."

Before she could ask what he meant, he pulled all the way out of her and hammered back inside.

"Oh!" she gasped.

He did it again and again. Pulling her whole body onto his as he fucked her hard and fast and deep. Over and over, shoving himself inside her and igniting sparks of pleasure that never died down.

Her breasts bounced, each movement causing them to spring farther and farther out of her bra, and the sounds of Jacob's hips slapping against her thighs rang through the shop, and the desk screeched and whined as he pounded her again and again.

She was whispering his name—wait . . . she was screaming it. Begging for more. Harder. She clawed at the desk beneath her, feeling like an animal and needing everything he had. Wanting him to slake it on her. Wanting to feel the heat and the anger and the passion.

She couldn't hold back. She didn't even have a warning for this orgasm. It hit her like a flash flood and swept her away with shocking force. She jolted so hard, she about came off the desk.

"That's it, baby," he said around gritted teeth. "I feel you squeezing me. You're going to make me come."

Just when she felt like she couldn't handle any more, Jacob shot impossibly hard and even larger inside her, spurring her orgasm into another dimension of amazing. She felt him come, strong and intense, just like he was.

He heaved over her, hanging his head for a moment to take in extra air. Her body was limp, spent, and so damn satisfied she didn't think she could walk.

Jacob pulled out of her, took care of the condom, and fastened his pants. He helped her up and pulled her skirt back into place as she fixed her bra and shirt.

Her legs were wobbly, so she had to lean against the desk to steady herself.

When she got the last button fastened, she looked at Jacob Lock.

And what a sight it was. Rumpled hair that her fingers had just been in and a lazy, happy smile took up his whole face.

"I guess it's true what they say," he said, running a hand through his hair. "Stopping to smell the roses really can brighten your outlook on the day."

Laura hit him with a glare, but it didn't hold any heat. Mostly because Jake knew exactly what real heat from the woman felt like now. Holy hell, he'd never come so hard in his life.

He'd wanted to make her beg. Show her how thorough he could be. And he had. Something he gave himself a mental high five for, because if it meant he'd get her to give in to him again, he'd take it.

She'd screamed—screamed—his name. Clawed at him and begged him. Those memories alone were going to keep him up all night for the foreseeable future. He wanted to prove a point, but he also wanted to learn her, in the only way she'd let him. Through sex.

"Why do you look so smug?" she asked.

He glanced at the mess of office supplies on the floor and the sexily disheveled hair she was rocking, and his chest puffed with pride.

"Just having a good day getting to know my coworker."

She glared at him again, and he couldn't help but kiss her quick as she rolled her eyes.

"We're not friendly. This was . . ."

"Thorough," he said. "We're business partners, you know. Pays to know the other's strengths and weaknesses. Likes and dislikes. For example, now I know you have a weakness for my mouth on you. And you like it both hard and slow."

"First off," she said, "we're not partners. We're stuck in this together for the moment."

"Oh, baby, I love it when you talk all logistically to me," he said sarcastically. "Especially since I just had you begging for me."

She moved past his words quickly. "Second," she said, "you have a weakness, too, and I think it's me."

He frowned. "I do not. It is not. And I'd love to tell you how much I don't have a weakness for you over dinner."

Great, now he sounded like a twelve-year-old. But the woman had him spinning. Making not-so-smart decisions and making him think of her in a way that wasn't good. Okay, it was good in that when he did think of her she was sprawled out in his bed, and all that hair she kept tied up was down and covering his chest—

Stop!

Not good.

She just smiled and glanced at the clock. "No dating. And thank you for your thoroughness, but I thought you were heading to the warehouse."

He growled low. She was trying to push his buttons with this whole owner-employee thing, and it was working.

"Enjoy your perch now, because sooner or later a strong breeze is going to blow you right onto that world-class ass of yours."

"I don't know about that," she said confidently. "This place is already looking better and gaining business."

"Well, whatever you need to do. Spend your money, get your flowers, but don't think this game of sexy boss versus man slave will last."

"Oh, I think you like being my man slave," she whispered low. "And Baughman Home Goods' money *is* my money, and I'll spend it how I see fit to enhance the business."

That made Jake pause. "Wait, you took from the business account for all this?"

She nodded. "Yes. These are business expenses."

"Laura, you can't do that."

"I can. My name is on the account."

"But you just got here. You know nothing about the books or what money is earmarked for, or the accounting. We can't write checks from the same till with different goals."

"And what checks are you writing, Jacob?"

His chest stopped. He didn't know where to begin with that.

"Everything!" he said. "This is a business, and money comes in and goes out, and now that you've taken from it, I have to get everything recalculated. You're leveraging the warehouse with every dime you spend."

"I'm tired of you thinking of this as separate. The shop is the warehouse, too. It's all connected."

This "thirty days waiting to see who would run Baughman" situation wasn't working.

"This is serious, Laura. You want the shop and warehouse to be together? Then act like it. The warehouse makes real money and employs real people. With families. I'm trying to run a business, pay employees, and keep inventory," he said and looked around. The amount of foliage that was now in the shop was extensive. She'd likely had it shipped overnight. And the new office fixtures? "How much did this cost, Laura?"

"There's plenty in the account—"

"How much?" he asked again.

"Five thousand."

Jake ran a hand through his hair. That was more than one of his guys' salary for the month. And coming up on a slow winter season, now was not the time to be spending five grand.

Yeah, Baughman Home Goods was well above water, but that's because he and Walt had built it up over a period of years. The steady build and steady income. He wasn't in the business of frivolous spending. Walt had taught Jake that he had to stretch the money he had, always keep reserves, and when a surplus came in, expect to have that last through the slow months. It wasn't just five grand—it was the fact that Laura didn't know any of this, yet she had the power to spend.

"The money needs to be back by the end of the week," he said.

"That won't happen," she countered, but her voice was a little softer. "But I already have a client lined up and I'll turn a profit on this event I'm doing. And I have extra flowers for the daily customers, and hopefully another reorder will come in and I won't have to scramble for inventory. I have a marketing plan, and I'm applying for Cal's subdivision project, too. It'll be fine."

"You're talking about risk and maybes."

"Sometime you have to risk to get the reward or you'll never get ahead. You'll tread water the rest of your life," Laura said.

Jake's chest tightened. He knew that feeling. Treading. He was good at it. But damn, his legs were getting tired with boredom. Still, he was responsible. He shook his head. "How much of a profit are you going to make on this first client?"

She glanced at the ground, not saying anything.

So he asked again. "Laura?"

"I gave Hannah the friends-and-family discount, because she only has so much money to work with and this is about building a reputation. It'll be more money in the long run, when her boss comes back to me for all their floral needs. Not to mention, the exposure at this party is great for business."

"Laura," he said, more deadpan. "What's the profit margin?"

"Forty-three dollars."

Jesus fucking Christ. "I can see that business degree is paying off."

"I have a degree in marketing, and it is paying off. I haven't been here that long and—"

"Are messing with the bank account," he said.

"I have a customer!"

The woman was infuriating. "This is your father's business. His legacy."

"I know that," she snapped. "But it's also my mother's flower shop and her memory."

And something in her eyes made him believe her. She was going about this ass backward, if you asked him, but she seemed genuinely aware that this business was Walt's, even though Jake never thought of her mother. About what came before him. And at least that was something. She was aware. He still had to think this through. They were fighting each other when all he wanted to do was be on her team. But the reality was, he couldn't be on her team. Because he was Team Warehouse and she was all or nothing.

"Well," Jake said and stepped around her, "like you said, I'm late for work." He walked out and toward the thing he'd built with Walt. The one place he could feel normal. The warehouse.

Chapter Nine

Laura had never thought she'd be a grown-ass woman pulling a wagon down Main Street of her hometown, but here she was, doing just that. The wagon had six medium flower arrangements in it that she was gifting local businesses today. She had the inventory, and sure, it was a couple hundred dollars' worth of flowers, but she needed the exposure and to gain a customer base.

Got to spend money to make money.

And after her fight with Jacob yesterday, she had to get more customers and fast. She was certain her idea was a sure thing. This town thrived on local business. Once everyone saw her mother's shop booming with flowers again, she'd have a line out the door.

She took a deep breath and continued her trek. The cobblestone sidewalk made the wagon wheels bump a bit, and she had to go slow so the flowers didn't jostle too much. Between the scraping of her stilettos and the squeaky wagon, she didn't exactly boast confidence. But as she reached Mr. Gaffe's taffy shop, she straightened her shoulders, parked her wagon near the entrance, grabbed an arrangement, and headed in.

"Good morning, Mr. Gaffe," she said and walked to the back counter. Both sides of the store were lined with candy. Each wall had a large display of built-in shelves that housed rows and rows of jars, all filled with different types of chocolates and sweets. But Laura's favorite was the big boat in the middle of the store—its simple wooden body had been hollowed out and rebuilt to hold bins of assorted homemade salt-water taffy.

"Little Laura Baughman, I was wondering when you and your sticky fingers were going to come see me," Mr. Gaffe said as she walked toward him. "That there is fresh butter taffy . . ." He motioned at the boat, then winked and closed his eyes. Laura took a single piece and popped it into her mouth. Butter taffy was her favorite, and ever since she was kid, she'd come in and Mr. Gaffe would pretend he didn't see her take a single piece every time.

"God, I've missed this place. And this taffy," she said, finishing the wonderful bite of smooth, buttery deliciousness.

"Well, we've missed you. Business dropped thirty percent after you left town," he teased. Sure, Laura had spent most of her money in the candy store, but she couldn't help it. Mr. Gaffe wore his usual pressed, all-white uniform, red bow tie, and matching paper boat hat. He looked like he'd stepped right out of 1955.

"Well, fear not, I'm back now and fully intend on spending a paycheck in here." That was, as soon as she actually had a paycheck.

"Happy to hear it. That's a lovely vase," he said, looking at the flowers. She set them gently on the counter near the register before him.

"Thank you. I'm running Baughman's floral shop, and I wanted to bring you a free arrangement."

"How kind," he said. He looked at the flowers and grabbed the vase, turned, and set it on the back counter, where the employees set their purses out of sight of customers. Which made her heart fall a little.

"I was hoping you could maybe mention where you got them if anyone asks?" Laura said. "I'm trying to grow my customer base. Let everyone know Baughman is back to selling flowers again."

"Of course," Gaffe said. But Laura felt like the importance of displaying the flowers where people could see them was lost on him.

"Maybe putting them by the register?" she asked.

"They smell lovely, child, but with the candy in here, I don't want to overwhelm the place with smell."

"Oh, right." Laura hadn't thought of that.

"I'll tell everyone, though," Gaffe said and smiled. Laura thanked him and left. Grabbing her wagon, she had five more stops to make on Main Street before she had to get back to the shop and load up the centerpieces for the party. At least the crew was at Baughman today and could help her.

Jacob wasn't an idiot. Okay, maybe he was, but only when it came to mouthy blondes from California. Because he was stupidly thinking about her for the millionth time that week.

He didn't know if she was avoiding him since their little sex session fight in the office—*excuse me, floral shop*—but he could bet she was. And he was kind of avoiding her, too.

But she'd been out of the shop more. Just today he'd caught a glimpse of her at Ron's Java Pit on the corner, handing him flowers. She was trying.

And he was, too. Trying to keep Baughman from losing any more money. His regular deliveries and working extra to prepare for the coming winter months were keeping his days long. Cal had called, and he'd sent it to voice mail. The man had to pick a foreman and supplier soon, and once he did and stopped holding out for Jake, he could finally stop avoiding him, too.

As always, Jake's mind turned to Laura. The Laura he could taste and touch but not date. She'd already lasted longer than he'd thought. Granted, when things started to get tough, she might still run. He was starting to really think she might stay. But things were about to get real tough. She kept wanting to lump the warehouse and shop together. She had no idea what came with that. She wanted a taste of what running the shop was like? Spending the shop's money? She needed to start seeing the *entire* shop, including the warehouse. Not just her magical oasis of snapdragons and daisies. Jake had no way to show that to her. It was easier said than done, and his head hurt trying to keep up with that woman and her ambition.

"Uncle Jake!" his niece Bella yelled and ran in his direction to give him a bear hug around the leg. It had been a whole week since he'd seen his sister last, and like clockwork, every Saturday morning, she came.

"Hey, doll face!" he said and lifted his niece up. Her six-year-old smile made his chest warm.

"I have bear claws!" his other niece, Lexi, announced. She was on her mom's heels, carrying a pink box. "They aren't from real bears, though. Just called bear claws."

"Good thing," Jake said and patted Lexi's head as she strutted by, heading straight for the table, clearly ready to devour the pastries in the box she was guarding.

He kissed his sister's cheek, happy to see the twins today and needing to regroup and refocus and figure out what the hell to do for this coming week. Priority number one—stop thinking about Laura naked. Priority number two—figure out a way to make Laura happy without losing any more of Baughman's warehouse money.

"You look grouchy this morning," his sister said.

He was. He glanced at the trailer. Everything that woman had ever said was lurking in his mind. Like the fact that his house was . . . what had she said? Sparse?

Everything looked sparse compared to her camper. Especially since he thought of how warm and inviting it was. Or how warm and inviting her body was.

His house was fine. His job was fine. So why was he seriously considering digging out his old Larry Bird poster from the garage and hanging it on the wall just to liven the place up a little? He then decided against it, because even if he could find the poster he'd had at thirteen, it probably didn't belong in a man's home.

It was a cool poster, though . . .

Maybe if he got it framed it would work better. Framed posters were classy, right? And Larry Bird was the best basketball player of all time. And then maybe Laura would come over and see he had some taste in art and then she'd want to hang out instead of saying things like how his house was empty and making him acknowledge she might have a point.

Priority number three—get Larry Bird poster framed and hung. Smart plan.

"How could I be grouchy with the two greatest sidekicks of all time right here?" He ruffled Lexi's hair right as she bit into her pastry. But neither she nor Bella looked thrilled.

"You're our sidekick, Uncle Jake. Bella and I talked."

"Ouch, so I'm demoted to Robin?"

"You can still have a bear claw, if that helps," Lexi offered.

"It does," he said and took a fresh claw from the box.

"Well, sidekick, any chance you can hang out with these two while I run to the clinic? There's a half shift needing coverage and . . ."

And she could use the extra money.

It was the one statement Erica said often, but never out loud. Because she said it silently with worry in her eyes. Jake knew her situation. She was a hard worker, raising two kids on her own and doing a damn fine job. And it tore at his heart that she took on extra shifts just to have a bit of financial wiggle room. He offered her money, help, anything, any time, but Erica was proud and would always take extra shifts before his money.

"Of course I'll watch them. My favorite nieces ever, after all."

"Aren't we your only nieces?"

"Yeah, and the best."

Bella preened. Lexi didn't care—she was way into her bear claw. They were a lot like Jake and Erica. The same in some basic ways, yet totally different with how they went about their personal situations.

"You're a lifesaver," Erica said and hugged and kissed the kids good-bye.

A few hours and peanut butter sandwiches later, Jake and his favorite kiddos were making an epic fort out of blankets and couch cushions when his phone rang.

"Hang on, Empress Master Fiend," he said to Lexi, who insisted she be called that when referring to her fort self. "This is Jake Lock," he answered his cell.

"This is Russ," the grouchy voice rang out.

"Hey, how's it going?"

"Well, not great, considering I don't have my sawdust that was supposed to be here an hour ago."

Jake frowned. His crew of four was working today to deliver the sawdust. It was the only delivery, and otherwise Mannie, his crew leader, was just going to oversee the warehouse today.

"I'm sorry, Russ, my guys should have been there." They never missed an order, especially one like Russ's—a recurring, large, and lucrative order.

"I'm sorry, too. Obviously your business is already going in the crapper. I need my supplies today, and if you can't deliver like you said you would, then I'll find someone else who will."

"I can," Jake said. "I'll have this straightened out and the sawdust to you this afternoon. I'm really sorry about this, Russ."

Russ grumbled and hung up, and Jake wanted to throw his phone. What the hell was going on? He called the shop, but it went to voice mail. Then he called Mannie, his lead guy, and got his voice mail, too.

"Okay, kiddos, you have to come with Uncle Jake to the warehouse for a minute," he said to the kids.

Packing them up, he got to the shop and it was dead. Not a soul in sight, and sure enough, Russ's sawdust was lying there, not even loaded on the truck.

"What the ever-loving hell?" Jake said, going through the warehouse. No one was there.

"You said a bad word, Uncle Jake," Bella said. Shit, he had.

"I'm sorry, sweetheart. Don't tell your mom."

He needed to find where his guys were and fast. Had something happened? Maybe they were at the job site with the gravel that was due Monday and got confused? Not likely, since this shipment was like clockwork every month, and Russ was one of their biggest moneymakers. But he had to start somewhere.

He didn't have time to look around for his crew, so he got his nieces some safe tools to play with—a.k.a. some Sharpies—and let them color on a two-by-four while he hopped in the bucket and moved the sawdust onto the dump truck in record time.

"Okay, who wants to ride in the big dump truck?" Jake asked, already sweating and thanking God he had a spare key to all the rigs at Baughman Home Goods on his key chain.

"Yay, dump truck!" the twins said. Jake hustled to get their car seats switched over to the truck and headed toward Russ.

Nothing about the situation was right. His anger was rising, and after having his ass chewed by Russ, only for Jake to smooth it out by offering a discount and ensuring this wouldn't happen again, he was back in the truck with the kids and pissed as hell. He'd never had to fire anyone before, but this was crazy. Mannie was his most trusted guy. So something had better be wrong, or Jake was going to lose it.

His afternoon was already shot, and Erica would be back at his place in an hour to get the kids. But once again, he had to go back to Baughman Home Goods to switch out rigs and get the kids back in his regular truck.

"It's like ring-around-the-rosy today, only with cars," Lexi said when Jake finally had them fastened in and heading back to his place.

"It really is, huh, kiddo?" He glanced in his rearview mirror and winked at his sweet nieces. "You two have been so good while I had to work. What do you say to some ice cream when we get back?"

Their little arms shot in the air and happy exclamations burst out.

Heading back through town, he was trying to tamp down the pissy confusion rising in his gut. He was going over what the hell he was going to say to Mannie when the SOB finally did call him back. But then Jake saw a Baughman Home Goods utility van—one of the vehicles they used to move tools and smaller lumber loads, especially when it was raining—parked outside Goonies. And wouldn't you know, there was Mannie's truck parked next to it.

So his crew was at a bar in the middle of the day, and that's why they'd missed an order?

Fuck. No.

Jake peeled out a little harder than he meant at the stop sign and parked at Goonies. His sister wouldn't love the idea of his taking the kids to a bar, but it was still before happy hour and lights out, and he had to figure out what was going on, so . . . the bar it was. Besides, there weren't any other cars in the lot, so it should be pretty empty inside.

Carrying Bella in one arm, he held Lexi's hand with the other and stomped toward the bar.

"Uncle Jake is mad," Bella said to Lexi. "Whoever Goonie is better watch out!"

Lexi nodded. "Yeah . . . Uncle Jake's muscles look angry."

Oh, Uncle Jake's muscles were very angry. It was time to figure out what the hell was going on.

~

"Thank you for your help, Mannie. You can set that last one right there," Laura instructed the crew who'd just unloaded the centerpieces. They were really great help today. Loading the flowers in the van, then driving them over and now setting up. Granted, she might have told them that she was the boss just as much as Jake was and needed their help, but it was only for an hour, two tops, and then they could go back to the shop.

The bar was closed for the party tonight. So aside from Laura and the crew, they were the only ones setting up, and it was going to look beautiful.

The door boomed open, and Laura jumped. She turned to see who had just entered the bar.

Oh my goodness . . .

Baby ducks were cute. Basket of puppies? Super cute. But the hulking Jacob Lock, covered in a light sheen of sweat and wearing a tight T-shirt, all rippled muscle, holding a pigtailed little girl in one strong arm and the hand of another blue-eyed girl in the other, was about the cutest damn thing she'd ever seen.

That was, until she caught the look in his eyes. Which appeared to be irate.

"What's going on here?" Jacob said, and the entire crew stilled like they'd been hit with some invisible freeze gun.

"Hey, boss," Mannie said and set the last centerpiece down and made his way to Jake. "We were just heading out."

"That right?" Jake said. She could tell by the strain in his jaw he was trying to hold back but was clearly pissed about something. "Heading back to do your job that you missed. Like Russ's sawdust order?"

"I'm sorry," Mannie said. "We had to help Miss Baughman."

Jake's eyes shot to hers. "The engagement party tonight," he said and looked around.

"Yeah," she replied. "How did you know about that?"

"My buddy Wayne is the one getting married, and I was invited."

A sting shot through her heart. Of course he was. The entire town loved Jacob Lock, and he was the kind of man that had an open invitation to anywhere.

"So let me get this right," Jake said to Mannie, and set the little girl in his arms down. "You blew off a job that brings in thousands of dollars a month from one of our longest-standing customers to bring flowers over here?"

Mannie's mouth dropped open, and he looked like he was ready to wet himself. Honestly, so was Laura. She'd never seen someone look so beyond angry. It was more than raw fury, it was disappointment. Which hit her own rib cage hard, and she felt the need to explain.

"I asked them to help me," Laura said, which was true. Okay, she'd told them, was more like it. "And they can still do the job today. It's not even three in the afternoon yet."

Jacob's icy eyes hit her. "You can't do this," he said.

That made her own anger rise and that fire she had been chasing burn hotter. Jacob needed to stop telling her what to do and stop underestimating her. "Yes, I can. They're my crew, too."

"No," he said. "They are people who work for Baughman Home Goods."

"Which I'm a part of."

"Don't you get it?" he snapped in a low whisper and closed in on her so only she could hear his words. "You won't have anything to be a part of if you keep this up. We'll go under."

"No, we won't," she said with shock. She'd seen the bank account. They were stable. In the black. Surely one order being late this one time wasn't an issue. Was Jacob trying to get a rise out of her? Scare her into his goals of always putting the warehouse first?

Well, she wasn't going to give in to that.

"The finances are stable. The cost analysis great. You just don't like that I have a different goal for Baughman Home Goods."

"You're right," he said. "I don't. Because it's not what your father would want."

"What he wants is for us to figure it out and show him who should run the entire shop as a whole," she snapped. Everything Jake and her father had built was wrapped up in the warehouse. Hell, it was wrapped up in Jake's house, too. But the flower shop was the only part that remained of her mother and her past, so she was clinging to it. The part she knew. The part that had anything to do with her and gave her hope. Because Jacob was right—she didn't know anything about the warehouse.

"Look," Jake said, clearly trying for calm. "Your little flower endeavor aside, it's bad business to be unreliable to your biggest client. He pulls his business and we're a grand shy from being in the red every month. We already have to earn back the five grand you took. That's a man's one-month salary, you know."

She swallowed hard. She had no idea that this one order brought in so much revenue. She'd never meant to cause a problem. She was trying to make this all work. Trying to take the business to the next level, to bring in *more* revenue, not less.

She wanted to say this to Jacob, but he'd already stomped away, clearly uninterested in anything she could have said.

"What the hell were you thinking?" he said quietly to Mannie.

She didn't know if Mannie was trying to keep quiet, but Laura heard him clear as day when he leaned in to Jake and said, "She's the boss, too, boss. We had to do as she said."

With that, Jake's eyes hit hers again, and she didn't like the feeling that came with being on the receiving end of a glare like that.

"We'll leave now to get the sawdust," Mannie said.

"Don't bother, I took care of it."

"*We* took care of it," the little girl with pigtails announced. "And we rode in the dump truck with Uncle Jake!"

Laura smiled. She was cute. And Uncle Jake had a nice ring to it. Made him softer than he was currently being at the moment.

"Uncle Jake?" the other little girl asked. "I'm hungry."

Jake nodded. "Let's get home then, kiddo."

Mannie and the guys followed him out, and no one said a word to her. Laura looked around at the empty bar. She was once again alone, only this time she was surrounded by flowers and wondering how badly she might have just screwed up, all while trying to figure out a way to stay above water.

Because if she was one wrong move away from sinking the company, maybe it, the town, and Jake were better off without her.

"No," she whispered and traced her finger along a dahlia perched on the vase nearby. The silky petal reminded her of when she and her mother had made bouquets from the garden every weekend. There wasn't a single dahlia that was alike. All so different in size, color, and composure. You never knew exactly what you'd get. Which was why she'd loved them. Why her mother had loved them. Why Walt had a garden full of flowers waiting for her mother. At least, he had before he'd sold it.

She just wanted to stop feeling so small. Her mother had been larger than life and the strongest woman she knew. The past ten years felt like a track she'd gotten lost on. And now Laura wanted to somehow feel her presence. Feel her love.

She couldn't give in yet. She had to try to make this work. Maybe if she just spent a bit of her time understanding the warehouse, made a calendar or something to keep track of all the orders so she wouldn't make this mistake again, everything would be okay. Her father would see she could run everything, and Jake would see she was capable. She also needed to show Jake she could bring in money and support herself and the shop.

She grabbed her phone and made the one call she'd been mulling over.

"Hi, Cal, this is Laura Baughman. I understand you're looking for a landscape designer and floral supplier for the new subdivision. I'd like to set up a meeting . . ."

She grabbed a pen out of her purse and wrote down the meeting time and date Cal suggested. This was her shot.

She glanced around again, her short breaths echoing in the stillness. And she didn't know if it was the drafty bar or the spot in her chest that was more hollow.

"I'm back!" Erica announced happily, walking into Jake's house. "How was your day?" she asked. Jake looked up from the coloring book he was working on with the kids at the kitchen table.

"Great!" the twins said in unison and ran toward her.

"It was a good day," Lexi said. "We rode in the dump truck to a bar so Uncle Jake could be mad at a pretty lady."

Erica's eyes went wide; then she glared at Jake. "What?"

Jake pinched the bridge of his nose. "It's not as bad as it sounds. The bar was technically closed."

That didn't seem to make Erica feel better. "Seriously, Jake?"

"I had no choice," he said. "Russ called and the sawdust didn't get dropped off, and I couldn't find my crew, so we took care of it."

"We?"

The twins nodded, and Bella piped up, "Yep! We helped. It was awesome."

"They were perfectly safe the whole time," Jake assured.

"Why don't you two go wash up and you can watch cartoons for a few minutes while I talk to Uncle Jake."

The kids ran down the hall, and Erica took a seat next to him.

"I'd never put them in danger," he said. And he meant it. Those kids and Erica meant more to him than anything.

"I know that," she said and nudged his arm. "I get that you have to work, but what's this about going to the bar to be mad at a pretty lady?" she asked. "Care to elaborate on that?"

"Not really," he said.

"Well, too bad, do it anyway."

With a deep breath, Jake replayed the situation and how he'd ended up staring at Laura Baughman at Goonies. While he left out the sleeping-with-her part, he did say that she was living in the camper outside.

"The woman is a pain in my ass, and it's getting worse," he said.

Erica smiled, clearly loving his torture.

"You like her," she said.

"Just a crush that dies hard."

"I've never seen you this riled over a woman before. *I* like her already."

Jake shook his head. "You're supposed to be on my side."

"I am. And I think you'd do a great job running the company, but Laura clearly doesn't know anything about the warehouse."

"Exactly!" he said. Finally someone was seeing things his way.

"Which is why she's working so hard at the floral shop, I bet. Think about it. That's what she knows. Just like you work so hard to avoid it. You stay in your comfort zone. It's human nature. Also a sign of stubbornness."

"Yes, she is stubborn," Jake agreed.

"I was talking about you, smart-ass."

Shit, Jake hadn't thought of that. He never took time for the flower shop because there was no point, and Walt had never seemed interested in it anyway. Come to think of it, Jake hadn't thought of a lot of things. Like why Walt seemed sad whenever it came to that part of the business. But Walt was happy when Laura was there running it. And he also hadn't thought of how her eyes had gotten so wide and her shoulders had sunk a little when he'd been harsh with her earlier today. But Laura

Baughman was tough. Nothing could get that woman riled, he was sure. Except riled for her claws to come out.

But hurt?

No way. She was strong. She was out to do her thing and driven as hell. Always had been.

"Whatever her reasons," Jake started, "it doesn't change the fact that she could seriously damage the business."

His sister nodded. "I know you care about Walt and the company, but she's his daughter."

Jake closed his eyes for a moment and heard the squeak of the fifth wheel outside. Laura was home, likely walking around in there. Maybe getting ready for the engagement party tonight? He didn't know, and he couldn't get sucked into her feelings or any of that. He had to treat this like a business. Because it was. Wanting her and lusting for her were different than *feelings*.

"You look like you're going to throw up," his sister said.

He might. He just might. Because he had the sneaking suspicion this wasn't going to get easier. He had three weeks until Walt would step in and make some kind of decision.

He needed a shower and at least a few beers to numb this kind of thinking. Good thing he was heading to a party at a bar tonight. Complete with booze, friends, and now flowers. Baughman Home Goods flowers.

He couldn't escape Laura's presence even if he tried.

Chapter Ten

Laura had spent the last few hours pacing in her camper, only to stop to sit down and work on a little home project.

After an hour and a glass of wine, she looked over her work of art and decided it was good enough. But she wanted it perfect.

So she grabbed one more flower, placed it in the vase, and . . .

"Yes!" She clapped happily at her work. She had a few flowers left over from the centerpieces and had decided to make her own arrangement.

Dusting her hands off on her jeans, she unrolled her long-sleeved sweater and glanced in the mirror, deciding quickly that she needed some lip gloss. Not that she had a big date or anything. In fact, she had zero plans other than finishing the bottle of Riesling in the fridge.

But she did have something she needed to make right.

With a final breath, she picked up the vase and walked out of her camper and up the porch steps until she was faced with Jacob's front door.

It seemed so quiet inside, but his truck was still there. So he couldn't have left for the party yet. She hoped the bar looked great and people liked the centerpieces. Part of her wished she could be there to meet people and try to give off some kind of good impression. Since she was coming up short lately in that department.

She knocked on Jacob's door and heard his heavy footsteps coming from the back of the house. Her heart picked up in pace and she gently tweaked one of the dark purple flowers when the door opened.

He was fresh out of a shower, and she was instantly engulfed with the spicy scent of his soap. He was clean shaven and wearing dark jeans and a red-and-black-checkered button-up that looked like it was made of soft flannel.

She wanted to touch him so badly to find out.

"Hey," he said and looked between her and the vase of flowers she held.

She cleared the cobwebs of lust away and held out her offering. "Having something alive in your house makes you live longer."

He grinned and took the vase. "My first choice would be for you to be in the house. For the sake of my health and all."

"I never said I want you healthy . . . ," she teased.

He laughed, and the deep, musical sound made her warm, and she smiled.

"This is really nice looking," he said, turning it in his hands to examine it. "You made this?"

"Yes."

He nodded and then leaned in to smell the flowers. He looked as if he actually appreciated the gift.

"They're beautiful. And so different."

"Actually, they're dahlias. All dahlias." She pointed to the large purple one, then to the smaller red one. "They come in different shapes and sizes, but they're the same flower. Which is why putting them together is so fun."

"You're clearly good at it, too," he said.

It was the first real compliment he'd given her regarding her work. And she liked how it made her chest feel a little fuller.

"I just wanted you to have that and to apologize for earlier today. I didn't realize the gravity of the delivery schedule, and I hope you didn't take it out on Mannie or the other men, because they were just doing what I asked."

She glanced at her feet, and her throat closed around the rest of the speech she'd prepared. Instead, her thoughts and words betrayed her.

"I want to do better. Be better," she said, not realizing she'd actually admitted that out loud until she saw Jacob's face. He was looking at her with a soft gaze.

Jacob looked like he was about to say something, but his phone chirped. "Sorry," he said and pulled it from his pocket and read a text. "I have to get going to the engagement party."

"Oh, of course," she said trying to sound as breezy as possible. Jacob set her vase down on a small table by the entry and then followed her out. He headed her off by his truck.

"Thank you for the flowers. They're really well done."

"You're welcome."

She turned to walk into the camper and he called out, "Come with me?"

"Excuse me?"

He walked up to the passenger side door of his truck and opened it, motioning for her to get in. "Come to the party with me."

"Oh, I wasn't invited."

"I'm inviting you," he said. "It'll be fun. And you'll get to see all your hard work enjoyed by others."

It would be nice to go. Not just to see if everyone did in fact like the flowers. But to be with Jacob for an evening. Like he said, showing a united front was smart. But deep down, she knew going with him tonight had nothing to do with the business. It had to do with him.

"I'm still not dating," she said, only she didn't sound convincing even to herself.

"Just dinner, flowers, dancing, and drinks. Nothing datelike about that," he teased.

It was then it hit her as hard as her smile. She liked Jake. A lot. He worked hard. Cared about her father and the business. And she respected him.

"Okay," she said and got in the truck.

The short drive was silent but not tense. As if both of them were lost to thought and neither broaching a subject of what a messed-up situation they were in. Sleeping together, working together, living together—kind of—and also technically in competition for their place at the business. Right now, he felt like a friend. One she wanted to spend time with. Confide in. Maybe kiss a little.

Okay, kiss a lot.

"It's like déjà vu," Jacob said, pulling into the parking lot of Goonies. It really was, since both of them had just been there earlier that afternoon.

"Hopefully circumstances are different tonight," she said.

He parked, turned off the truck, and turned to look at her. "They are." With his hand resting on the back of the seat, he trailed a fingertip along her ear, gently tucking a piece of her hair behind it. "You never need to be anything better than what you are," he said softly.

She looked into those blazing blue eyes, and the warmth in her chest bloomed another degree.

"Many people would disagree," she said.

"Then they're idiots."

She glanced at her hands in her lap and gently shook her head. It took her a full minute to work up the guts to say what they both knew was true. "I may be my father's daughter, but he loves you, Jacob." She gave a sincere smile. "How could he not? You're something special. And you run the warehouse really well. Have for a long time, while I wasn't here."

She opened the truck door and got out, and Jacob called her name and rounded the truck to catch her just as she closed the door and walked toward the bar.

"Hey, Laura, let's talk about this."

She shook her head. "There's nothing to talk about. I'm sorry about today. I'll try harder, and maybe we can figure out a schedule or peace treaty or whatever that can work for both of us."

She started for the bar again, but he grabbed her hand. "I mean, let's talk about what you said."

"Not tonight. Please." She glanced between him and the rowdy bar, where music was blaring and people were laughing and talking. "I'm here now. I can't make up for the mistakes of the past. And things are the way they are. I don't want to dive into things I can't change." She also wasn't in the mood to admit out loud how lacking she'd become in the past decade. How she was trying to build her self-esteem back. How badly she wanted to do something right by her mother's memory, by her father, by herself.

"Can you just take me inside and enjoy the night?" she asked, and if she were honest, there was a slight plea in her voice.

"Yeah, of course," Jake said, and with a hand on the small of her back, he led her to the bar and inside.

Music and people and commotion were all in full swing. And the flowers on all the tables and gave pops of color to the entire room; Laura saw a woman lean in and look at one centerpiece closely, then nod happily to her friend and point.

Looked like a good review.

She turned to tell Jacob and realized that he'd gotten swallowed by a crowd of people giving him slaps on the back and talking his ear off. One guy handed him a beer. The man hadn't even made it all the way in the door yet and he was engulfed like a celebrity.

Must be hard being so well liked . . .

He met her eyes and tried to make his way toward her, but she shook him off with a smile and motioned that she'd be around. They weren't dating—no reason they had to stay together. So she wandered around, checking on the vases. The flowers were holding up nicely, and after getting a glass of wine from the bar, she settled in a corner and watched.

She didn't fit in. She knew it. Thank God she was in jeans and a sweater, at least, since she was learning quickly that the standard attire around Yachats was casual. At least she didn't stick out in a bad way, but she wasn't embraced like Jacob. Not that she expected to be, after she'd only been in town for a couple of weeks. No, what worried her was that she might never be embraced.

"Hello there again," a sweet older woman's voice called.

"Tilly?" Laura said as the woman came to stand by her. "I haven't seen you since book club."

"You've kept up with the reading?" Tilly asked.

"Not exactly," Laura admitted. She'd been busy with the shop, not to mention having her own steamy scenes with Jake.

"Well, that's all right. We'll catch you up. I see you've been busy. These centerpieces are lovely."

"Thank you," Laura said. She was glad she knew a friendly face.

The old woman smiled and looked around. "I'm so glad that you're reviving that shop. Your mother would have been proud."

Breath stuck in Laura's lungs. The idea that her mother would have been proud was a gift to the goal she'd been chasing. And yet, it hurt as much as it warmed her entire chest. Because she wanted to make her proud. So much. Almost as much as she missed her.

"Thank you," Laura said softly. "I'm happy to be doing it." She looked at Tilly. "I'm glad you're here, too."

"Well, I have to be, dear, I'm the mother of the bride."

"Congratulations!" Laura said, happy for her. Tilly ran a hand through short gray hair. Her smile was one of pride and dark purple lipstick.

"My daughter hasn't picked a florist yet for the wedding, you know?"

Laura's eyes went wide with shock and happiness.

"I could give her your card?" Tilly offered.

Embarrassment set in. "I don't have a business card yet. But I can give you the number to the shop or you can come by anytime. I'd love to chat with you and your daughter about what she's looking for."

Tilly smiled and nodded. "That'd be great. I'll check with her schedule and we'll pop in. In the meantime, try to get some reading in. You look like you could use some good fiction."

Laura smiled. Just as Tilly turned to leave, she mentioned, "I work over at the senior center. We could sure use something pretty in the entryway. Maybe a fresh large arrangement once a month?"

"Yes," Laura said with excitement. "I'd be happy to put together some options and work with you."

"Do you deliver and set up?" She glanced around the bar.

"Yes, absolutely."

"That would be wonderful, then!" She leaned in and nudged Laura's shoulder. "I have a budget of two hundred dollars a month for office upkeep, and I think that brightening up the place with some flowers is the way to go."

"Tilly, thank you so much."

"Don't thank me, you earned it. Look around you. You're the woman behind this beauty."

It was the one of the kindest things she'd heard in a while and exactly what Laura needed right then. Tilly waved to someone across the room.

"I'll see you soon, dear," she said.

"Yes, I look forward to it," Laura said, and Tilly waved back to her as she walked toward a group of women calling her over.

Laura glanced at the centerpiece on the closest table and felt a twinge of pride. Not for what she'd done, but because someone remembered her mother, remembered the shop when it sold flowers, just like Laura remembered. And Laura had just been hired on merit. On her work and her flowers.

Maybe she could keep her mother's memory alive in a way after all. Jacob had the warehouse and everything he and her father had built together. Maybe this missing piece really was Laura's to carry on. A part of her mom that she could build on. Success to earn.

The music slowed and several couples were dancing in a large spot in the center of the bar that had been cleared of tables. It really felt like a community here. Everyone knowing everyone. Laughing and enjoying themselves. Laura wished Hannah was here so maybe she'd have someone to talk to. But no luck.

"Pretty thing like you in the corner by yourself is a shame," Jacob said, coming to stand by her and looking at the same crowd she was.

"Aren't you just full of flattery," she said.

He shot her a wink and took a drink of his beer. There was a casual air between them. Calm. Playful.

Between the almost admission and half details about her past, plus the secret sex she'd been having with Jacob and the not-so-secret fights that came before and after, she didn't really know what they were. Surely not together. But not really enemies, either.

"Looks good in here," he said and pointed to a centerpiece. "But I have to admit, I think I have the best one at home."

"Yours was the cheapest to make," she teased.

"Still the best," he said with a grin. He set his beer on the bar behind them and took her glass of wine and set it down as well.

"What are you doing?" she asked.

"Well, I'm looking to do a lot of things, but I wanted to start with a dance." He held out his hand, and for the first time since she'd gotten to that small town, she felt wanted.

At least for a moment.

She took his hand, and he led them to a spot on the floor. He twirled her once and pulled her back. She laughed and enjoyed that little spin and then settled close, her hand in his, while he led her around the floor with a strong palm on her side.

"You should do that more often," Jacob said against her ear.

"Do what?" she asked.

He spun her out again, twirling her, and another laugh broke free right as he tugged her close once more.

"Laugh," he said. "You should laugh more."

She smiled up at him. "There's a lot I should do more of."

"I hope I'm on that list," he said with a wink.

"No, you're not."

"Ouch." He faked sadness, but they both knew all he had to do was get her in a private room with his mouth on her and she'd likely turn into a puddle for him.

"I have a new customer—Tilly. She's the mother of the bride," Laura said.

"Yeah, she's a good lady. I'm glad you're drumming up more business."

"Me, too, but you're right. I need to look at Baughman Home Goods as a whole, not just the flower shop. Which is why I have an idea."

"Oh?" he asked and pulled her a little closer, keeping perfect stride with the music. "Let's hear it."

"I want to be your shadow," she said.

"I'm liking where this is going."

"I mean at work. I want to see what you do in the warehouse, and learn."

He leaned back to look her in the eyes with seriousness. "Really?"

"Yes, this is important to me. I don't want to mess up orders like today, and I need to know what you boys do out there all day so I can make smart, well-informed decisions."

Jacob thought for a moment. "So you want to shadow me? Looking but no touching?"

"I suppose I could get my hands a little dirty," she said.

"Oh, baby, you keep talking like that and I may have to take you home with me."

Laura laughed when he twirled her again, and she couldn't help but hope that his offer was a serious one.

～

"Thank you for a lovely evening," Jake said, trying for sweet date material and coming off goofy. But it was making Laura smile, so he'd keep acting like a damn fool if it meant he got that pretty grin aimed his direction.

"Thank you for the ride," she said, swaying a little in front of the camper door. "And thank you for walking me to my door."

"Anytime," he said.

"Would you like to come in?" she asked.

Jake paused, and his first thought was hell, yeah, he did. He couldn't handle walking away from her tonight. It had been so good. And so heavy. There was more to Laura Baughman than he'd ever realized. He just wasn't sure how to go about tapping into that.

Because it was clear she was trying. It was also clear there was strain between her and whatever she was outrunning from her past. And Jake wanted to know. Wanted to know her. Wanted to know about her.

"I would," he said, "but I probably shouldn't, since I'm not so great with look-but-don't-touch rules."

Laura opened the door and walked in. She looked at him over her shoulder and smiled. "Who said that you couldn't touch?"

That was all it took and Jake was on her heels in a split second. He got into the camper and shut the door behind him. It was small but cozy and he was happy to be inside. To get a glimpse of her world. Be a part of it. Feel the warmth.

She sat on her small bed; the thing looked comfy but not overly large.

Laura seemed to get what he was staring at, and she shifted to look straight up at him, her face eye level with his belt.

"You look about as big as my bed," she said. And yep, she could read minds, because Jake was thinking the same thing. "But I feel like I need to really see the whole package to be sure . . ." She lifted her chin at him. "Strip, please."

He frowned down at her. "What?"

"You heard me. Unless you'd rather go home? Otherwise, get naked, because I'm in the mood to see all of you."

Jake couldn't really say no to that. "Be warned, I expect an equal trade."

"Fair enough," she agreed.

He couldn't help but grin. Even gearing up for foreplay with her was a challenge and fun. He reached behind his head and tugged off his shirt, pulling it down his arms and off.

Her eyes went wide as she stared at his chest and trailed those topaz gems down to his stomach and back up again.

"Whoa, I knew you were strong, but this . . ." She looked him over again. "You're so . . ." She ran a hand from his nipple down his torso to his belt and back up again. She seemed transfixed by all the ridges of his stomach, and Jake couldn't help but want her eyes to stay on him.

He wanted her to want him.

Loved how her mere gaze made him feel stronger.

"Your skin is soft," she said, running her hand along the V of his hips then up his side. "But you're hard muscle beneath."

The woman was staring at him like he was a damn Greek god or something—like she was impressed with him, wanted him—and holy shit, he liked it.

"You know the taffy stretcher down at Gaffe's shop?" she asked.

Jake frowned at her question.

"It's a rotating wheel that pulls and stretches saltwater taffy. Hard and soft. Smooth and dense. I used to watch it at the candy shop by the wharf when I was a kid, and every time I wished so much I could just taste it. It looked so damn good."

She leaned in, and her breath hit his belly button. With her palms flat on his upper torso, she pressed her lush mouth against his skin. Her lips on him made him groan, and when her tongue darted out to taste him, he gritted his teeth. His cock shot impossibly hard in his pants, and never once had a woman gotten him so turned on while his pants were still on.

"Jesus, baby," he said.

"Finish your task," she said, keeping her mouth on his abs.

Jake didn't want her mouth to leave him, so he gently reached down to unfasten his belt and jeans while she licked along his hips.

He tugged his pants down, and with her perfect face right there, his cock sprang free.

She wasn't retreating. Wasn't moving away. She just kept taking tastes of him, and when the side of her cheek brushed his cock, he bit back a curse.

She was so close. So damn close to where he prayed her mouth would end up. But he didn't want to rush her.

"You know what?" she said and looked up at him. "I think I want to taste you more than the taffy."

Thank God!

She kept her eyes on him, and he watched her plump lips part and fasten around his cock head.

He had to take a shuddering breath, because he'd never seen anything sexier than this woman. Running her hands up his abs, she slowly sucked him deep while gently scratching a trail back down to his pelvis. When she came back up, so did her hands. She was working him over in a slow, steady way while keeping her hands and mouth on him at all times.

And he loved it.

But when her hands came around to grab his ass, nothing prepared him for her. She gripped him tight and pulled, bringing his hips forward and causing him to fuck her throat.

She sucked and moaned as she pulled him toward her again and again, and Jake thought he'd died and gone some kind of kinky heaven, because this was amazing.

She was taking him deep and clawing at him for more.

He flexed his hips just enough to gauge her comfort, and she went wild. Sucking harder, tugging him closer.

"Baby, you're so good. I don't want to hurt you."

But she just kept demanding more, and Jake couldn't resist. He threaded one hand in the back of her hair and the other gently cupped her throat as he began to thrust into her eager mouth.

She moaned in approval, so Jake kept up his pace. He'd never been so close to exploding in his entire life. But he held out as long as he could. As amazing as this was, he wanted to come while he was buried inside her.

He pulled away, and she instantly huffed. "Don't go," she said.

"Oh, I'm going somewhere," he said and reached down to tug her sweater over her head and off. "And it's inside you."

He unsnapped her jeans, and as she lay back on the bed, he grabbed the pants and yanked them off her.

Almighty, she was a sight. In nothing but white lace panties and matching bra, her long tan legs looked smooth and soft. He was seeing the affinity for taffy now and just wanted to taste it. Run his tongue along her thigh and up her flat belly. But when she held up her arms, reaching for him, he was a goner.

He kicked off his pants the rest of the way, stopping only to grab a condom from the pocket and cover himself before nestling between her thighs.

"Since this bed isn't big enough for both of us, you'll have to stay on top of me," she said with a smile.

"Or you on top of me," he said.

"I am the boss, after all. Me on top does make more sense . . ."

He pinched her nipple gently, and she gasped, then smiled. "Oh, you don't like that, huh?" she said. "Want to show the boss lady just how strong you are?"

He reached between them and moved her panties aside with his cock, then placed it at her opening.

"We both know how strong I am," he said with a growl. "You just need to start admitting how bad you want me."

He thrust hard inside her and watched her face split with pleasure and shock; her sexy little gasp made him want to hear it again and again. So he withdrew until only the tip was in and pounded back inside.

"I can't hear you now, boss," he said. "Weren't you going to tell me how much you wanted me?"

He fucked her again and again. In and out, gasp after gasp.

"Yes, yes, Jacob. I want you."

"You want me hard like this," he asked, shoving deep and watching her breasts bounce so hard they spilled from the bra she was wearing, which barely covered her to begin with. Something he was really happy about.

He bent his head to take a sample of a pouty nipple just begging to be sucked. And he was happy to oblige.

She gripped him closer, wrapping her arms around his back while locking her legs together around his hips. Like she wanted him to stay close. As she hugged him impossibly hard, he could feel all of her strength. He felt not just wanted but, in that moment, needed.

He slid his arms under her and pulled down on the top of her shoulders as he thrust. Because he wanted her closer, too. Deeper. More.

There was no space between them. His chest pressed heavy on her breasts and her hard nipples poked his chest in the best way, giving him jolts of joy as they teased his skin.

Her sweet lips parted and she breathed shallowly and quickly. Every time he surged home, she gasped a little, and he wanted to catch that sexy sound with his own mouth.

He flicked her top teeth with his tongue, and she opened wider. He took advantage and slid his tongue in, drinking her down in one long, hot kiss.

He could have sworn she'd said his name around that kiss. But she couldn't have, because he was consuming her. Taking deep draws from her addicting lips and refusing to let her get away.

He rocked harder, picking up the pace but staying deep until she was panting with him. Breathing for him. Her little claws dug into his back, and her sheath squeezed his cock hard. She was close. He was learning her body already, responding to it. Knew right where she was. He also knew that if he slid deep, then flexed his hips up like this—

"Jake!" She cried his name and came apart around him.

"That's it, baby," he whispered against her mouth. "Let me feel you."

And he did feel her. Everywhere. From her tight sex milking his cock to her nails scratching his back to her laugh still ringing in his ears and her entire presence taking up space in his chest. He felt her.

He was right there with her and couldn't hold back. He buried himself deep and stilled just enough. He came hard, felt every lash of his release leave him, and twitched against the inside of her. She caught him. Held him. Arched and kissed him as if silently begging for more.

His skin pricked with goose bumps as he followed her over the edge of the abyss. He was pretty sure there was no going back.

Laura's whole body moved as if she was experiencing an earthquake. She peeked one eye open just as she felt the warm blanket she'd been wrapped in untangle and leave her chilled.

But it wasn't a blanket or an earthquake. It was Jacob unwinding his big body from hers. The camper swayed a bit as he put on his jeans, then his shirt.

"You're leaving?" she asked, trying to clear the sleep from her voice. How long had she been out? She remembered melting into a puddle for Jacob and then feeling so safe in his big arms she just got lost in him.

"Go back to sleep, baby," he said in a soft whisper. "I'm going to make coffee and I'll come check on you here in a bit."

She frowned, but she was exhausted. And her mind was already trying to churn out what last night had meant. Probably nothing—it was just sex, after all. First time they were lying down and more intimate, but that didn't mean they were friends or more or . . . anything.

She needed to get her mind focused on something other than Jacob Lock. Otherwise silly questions, like Does he like me? and Do I like him? would start to creep in. And she already knew the answer to the latter, which was why his leaving was probably best.

"Rest up, you have a big day tomorrow." He leaned over and kissed her forehead.

"Big day tomorrow?" she asked.

"Yeah, Monday. We get the lumber order in and you wanted to be my shadow, right?"

She nodded.

He bent and kissed her again, only this time on the mouth. And she couldn't help but kiss him back.

"Then be prepared for some heavy lifting, baby."

With a smile and a last playful smack on the lips, he walked out and into the dawn.

She had twenty-four hours to figure out what the hell she was doing before taking on yet another aspect she didn't quite understand: the warehouse.

Before she could groan, her phone rang.

She reached for it on the bedside table and answered.

"This is Laura Baughman."

"Hello, this is Jill with LA Marketing. I'm calling to schedule an HR appointment to go over the paperwork for your new job."

Laura frowned. "I'm sorry, new job?"

"Yes, we sent you an e-mail with the acceptance letter and the hiring package last week. I wanted to call to follow up with you."

Laura's eyes shot wide. She'd applied for a few jobs in California last month, but after several interviews, she hadn't thought she'd gotten any of them. LA Marketing was a huge firm near Los Angeles, and they were offering her a job!

She glanced toward the door, where Jake had just left.

"I'm sorry, I've been away . . ." She thought of the computer at the shop and had a sneaking suspicion that spam was the issue.

"Okay, well, if you're interested, we'd like to invite you to come tour, go over paperwork, and get you started. Are you free next week?"

Laura couldn't kill a bird in the bush or in her hand at this point. Her father was supposed to make a decision soon about the fate of the shop and Laura's place around here. Since she didn't technically have job security here, keeping her options open was smart.

"Yes, next week is great," she said. It didn't mean she'd take it. It meant she was keeping her opportunities close. Because she wanted to build a life here, and she was, but she was currently in the red. And if she failed and her father let Jake be the head honcho, and he cut off the warehouse money, she couldn't keep the store afloat on its own. She either had to get some business, turn a profit, and land the big contract with Cal, or she might have no better option than going back to California and taking this job. A safety net was always wise.

Chapter Eleven

He'd thought leaving Laura in bed twenty-four hours ago was tough. But watching her walk into his warehouse today, ready to work, was hot.

She looked hot as hell, and if those were her getting-dirty clothes, Jake didn't want to know what dressing up for her was. He loved her sexy skirts and crisp tops. She always looked big-city business in those. And jeans were a fine look for her, too. Maybe a prom dress at this point was fancy for her, because he had yet to find something the woman didn't look amazing in.

She was in sleek black jeans and tight white shirt, which hugged all her curves in the right spots, and he couldn't help but stare. She wore red lipstick and her hair fastened back, and he looked down to find . . .

"No red heels today, huh?"

Instead, there was a pair of black Converses on her feet, and they looked about the cutest thing he'd ever seen.

"You said work clothes. So I couldn't very well wear heels," she said.

"Indeed," he agreed. After a quick intro to the crew once again, he went into what he did best—running the warehouse. If Laura really wanted to see how all this worked, he had to stay true to the routine.

"Okay, so the lumber order is coming in today and we have to unload it when it gets here. First, we have to move this gravel onto the truck, and then Mannie will take it to a customer." Jake showed Laura the paperwork, the schedule, and how the warehouse kept track of what supplies came in and what went out.

"Okay," Laura agreed and looked at the heap of gravel. "So all this"—she motioned to the mountain—"goes on a dump truck?"

Jake nodded. "Yep."

She blew out a breath and looked around. Her eyes fastened on a tin bucket Jake had used to catch a leak in the roof last year. She picked it up and walked over to the gravel pile. With her chin held high, she scooped the bucket full of gravel, then went to the dump truck and hoisted it inside.

Jake chuckled a little, and she turned to glare.

"Unless you have a better way or a bigger bucket, I suggest you stop laughing at me."

"Fair enough," he said. "You want to see a bigger bucket?" He went to the loader machine, hopped in, and started it up. Rolling toward the gravel, he got a large scoop and took it to the truck. It would only take four more scoops and it'd all be loaded.

Laura glanced at the bucket in her hand and then tossed it and nodded.

"Quit showing off," she yelled at him and then smiled. She wasn't totally immune to his charms, and honestly, he wasn't immune to hers, either.

He finished loading the gravel, trying to concentrate on the task and not on the other night with Laura. How being with her had felt different. She was also trying. She'd showed up ready to work. Was looking around and watching Jake. She talked to the crew and looked through supplies.

Between getting the gravel out and the lumber in, the day was flying by pretty quickly, and Laura didn't complain once. But things were about to get trickier as Jake walked her through the different wood sizes and how they organized and stacked them all based on orders they had prepared for.

She just listened, asked questions, and was genuine in trying to learn.

"Here's the manual labor part," he said, standing by a wall of newly delivered lumber. "Machines help with some of this, because we need to move the larger pieces with some smaller pieces depending on the delivery we have coming up. No sense organizing and reorganizing it, so we try to plan what is going out and to whom and have that order ready to go."

"Makes sense," she said.

"Which means Henry Davis's order is here." He pointed at the clipboard he had along with the various sizes of wood Henry had ordered. "We're going to stack his order against the wall right there." Jake pointed to the east side of the warehouse. "So when we have to load it and deliver it next week, we already have it ready to go."

"Okay," Laura said, nodding in understanding.

"I'll use the machine to get the bulk of the order, but if you want to work with the guys on walking over the smaller pieces, you can do that."

"Will do," she said with a smile, but Jake could tell she was dragging a bit. This was hard work. But she was doing it. They all worked together to get the wood organized, and Laura kept pace the entire time.

Jake was more than impressed—he was certain now that he'd been wrong about her. She was staying. Laura Baughman was done running. And he was ready to risk a hell of a lot for her.

Laura watched Jake use heavy machinery all day, and holy hell, he was sexy. All those muscles working and the effortless ease with every move he made had her panting. He was in his element. Confident. And she could see why her dad trusted him. The shop was in good hands with him.

He was patient with her, too, showing her how the warehouse operated and answering her questions. He really did have this job down, and if she were honest, she hated this. Moving wood was not her idea of fun. She wanted to get back to her flower shop, with a new respect for what went into this part of the business.

A twinge of guilt flooded her.

If Jake was right, and the warehouse brought in the majority of the revenue for Baughman Home Goods, she'd have to get on board real quick. Otherwise the company would suffer. And maybe Jake was better to oversee it all than she was.

She really had no idea what she was doing when it came to this aspect of the company. She was learning, but she'd never be as good as Jacob. And she didn't want to be. He clearly loved his job and was amazing at it. She loved the floral shop. Overseeing all the men and the orders and moving lumber wasn't her expertise and wasn't enjoyable.

What the hell kind of owner was she trying to be, then? She didn't even like the main part of the business. But the idea of leaving the floral shop behind made her chest throb. She was finally making headway with it, integrating into the community a little and building a life. She was finding happiness. And she didn't want to give that up. But she couldn't chase any of those things at the expense of the business, or Jacob.

She thought of the California job. Of her mother's memory. Of her father's retirement and the fate of Baughman as a whole. It was so much responsibility, and it was hers to lose. To fail.

Maybe she should think harder about California . . .

Jacob chatted with the crew, and the men dispersed in several directions, some handling the distribution of the gravel, and the others off to various tasks. That was, whatever Jacob instructed them to do. She, however, felt sweaty, her hands ached from carrying the wood, and she had a nasty splinter.

It was break time.

Because while she felt gross, Jake just looked hot. And not in temperature.

She wound through the massive warehouse until she found a quiet spot in back near a small counter that housed a lone coffeepot. She stared at the concrete floor.

Leaning against the wall, she took one long inhale . . .

"You all right?" Jacob asked, weaving around pieces of machinery she didn't know the names for and coming to stand in front of her.

"Yes," she said and gave her best smile. "Just taking a quick breather."

Surrounded by heavy machinery in the corner and the smell of fresh-cut lumber, her hormones ignited when Jake looked her over.

His jeans were dusty, his T-shirt tight over his muscles, and holy God, the man was built and strong and sexy. And as Jake came toe to toe with her, she realized that she really did need to breathe. Preferably with his mouth against hers.

She reached for him, cupping the back of his neck and yanking him down for a kiss. He instantly responded and pushed her against the wall, devouring her mouth.

"Looks like I need a breather, too," he said and nipped her bottom lip.

She unfastened his belt and tugged on his pants. She didn't know what came over her, but she did know she had to have him. Had to feel his skin. Had to feel all his strength wrapped around her.

This was happening, and she was beyond ready. She was frantic. Clanging her teeth against his as she tried to kiss him hard while tearing at his clothes. Damn, she needed him.

"What's gotten into you?" Jake asked but kept busy working her pants open. He seemed just as desperate for her.

"Don't know. You on a big machine is hot, I guess." She got his belt open and his cock free. She gripped him tight.

He growled and tore her pants off and kicked her feet apart.

Grabbing a condom from his pocket, he put it on quickly, then hoisted her up and plunged inside her. Her legs wrapped around his hips, and she cried out his name.

"You're so sexy working hard, you know that?" he said and thrust inside her again.

She held on tight. Just like the other night. Just like every night when it came to Jacob in her world.

"I was just thinking the same thing about you."

The rain started, and it pounded the tin roof above, creating a pretty echo and loud dinging sound.

He fucked her against the wall, hard and fast. His mouth stayed on hers as he took her body to the brink in record time. With the sound of the storm brewing around them, there was no fondling, no sweet kisses or exploration of bodies. This was sex against the wall. Rough and wild and consuming.

With every hard thrust Jacob gave her, her ass banged against the wall and she cried out louder and louder. Her body started to crackle with the impending orgasm that was just out of reach.

The sound of the dump truck returning echoed through the warehouse. Mannie was back from the gravel delivery and near the front of the shop, while Jake had her pinned against a corner in the back.

Oh God! They were going to get caught.

She tried to scramble away, but Jake didn't let her budge. Instead, he put a hand over her mouth and thrust harder.

Her eyes went wide.

"You're coming for me, baby," he said quietly.

His strength and determination surrounded her and with every deep glide, every punishing thrust, he took her so deeply that her back slid up the wall.

She couldn't deny him. The fire spread from her sex to her breasts, burning up her blood as her release shot through every single vein.

She screamed against his palm, and he just fucked her harder. Through her orgasm and into another one while he found his release.

His breath was heavy in her ear as he groaned her name and she felt him tense and come, his big body shuddering against hers.

He slowly peeled back his hand and peppered kisses across her mouth, her nose, and her cheek, finally letting her slide down while he cleaned up.

"Boss?" Mannie called. His footsteps came closer. "Boss, you back here?"

Laura moved double time to tug her pants on and fix her hair and try not to panic. Jake just looked cool and collected. He simply fastened his belt and watched her.

She made a gesture in Mannie's direction.

"Hey, I'm back here," Jake called out.

"What the hell are you doing?" she whispered.

"What? You're dressed."

"I'm frazzled!" she whispered, harsher this time.

"You're beautiful," he said, just as Mannie walked up. "Hey, how did the delivery go?" Jake asked him, as if nothing had just happened.

"Great. Straightforward."

"Excellent. You can take off for the day if you want, after we go over tomorrow."

"I'll be up front," Mannie said, then nodded to Laura and turned to leave.

Jacob just turned to her, gave her a kiss, and smacked her butt. "That was the best damn breather I've ever had."

He gave a smile that made her mouth dry and other areas wet. She watched him walk back toward the front of the shop, and she knew right then that she was in big, big trouble. Because not only was she growing increasingly worried that she couldn't run the warehouse anywhere near as well as Jake could, she was also falling for the sexy foreman and worst, it was affecting her heart.

Chapter Twelve

"This is going to be real nice, Cal," Jake said to his buddy, looking out at several acres of land ready to be built on.

"The plans are all drawn up, and this whole area will have rustic-looking log cabins instead of the cookie-cutter houses you normally get with subdivisions."

"It'll look great, man." Jake slapped his buddy on the back. He'd known Cal a long time. And the man not only worked hard but was talented. The homes he built were unique. He'd started a small construction company once upon a time and now had a major contract and his own crew.

"Yeah, and you'll be the lumber supplier, right?" Cal nudged his shoulder.

"Still haven't hired someone yet?" Jake said. Which made his buddy face him with a serious look on his face.

"I have to, Jake. I can't wait any longer," Cal said. "I hear with Laura working there, you can be freed up more. Take this project. Work with me on it."

Jake couldn't do this right now. He was thinking of Laura and how the time was coming for Walt to step in. "Speaking of Laura, I heard she went for the supplier and marketing job. She's great and really talented. You want to work with someone, it's her."

Cal shook his head. "She's great. But I'm going with someone else from Lincoln City."

"What?" Jake said in shock.

"Cheaper and more experienced. It's nothing personal."

But it would be to Laura. She'd worked so hard, and this rejection from Cal wasn't good for business. Jake knew the hole she was in. She was pretty much banking on this contract. Otherwise, with small orders here and there, it would take her a while to dig out of the red ink she was currently swimming in.

"What would it take to get her the contract?" Jake asked.

Cal frowned then raised his brows. "You."

Jake was silent. He had a feeling. Then he did the only thing that felt right—and wrong at the same time.

"You want me, I come as a package deal. Laura, too."

"Seriously?" Cal said with shock. His friend looked at him. "What the hell has gotten into you?"

"What?" Jake said.

"You've been fighting me on this and now you're ready? Because of a woman?"

"Not a woman, the right woman. For your job, I mean. She can do it; she just needs a chance."

"So you're not worried about the business? Especially when word spreads that you've been slacking at Baughman."

"We're not slacking," Jake said immediately. But he knew what his buddy was referring to. Russ's mouth was bigger than his beard, and he clearly didn't like Laura. He was likely still pissed about the delay in delivering his order last week. Even with a 20 percent discount and free delivery for his next two orders, apparently the old man was still running his mouth.

"Everything is fine. Solid," Jake said. "Now do you want the deal or not?"

Cal looked him over. "You're my foreman for six months and lumber supplier for the project?"

Jake nodded. "So long as Laura is also your supplier and landscape designer."

Cal held out his hand to shake Jake's. "Deal."

Laura was just putting the finishing touches on the arrangement that would be the start of a monthly order for the senior center.

Tilly had called her a few days ago, and after a meeting and some paperwork, Laura officially had a regular customer. She was still set to go to California at the end of the week, but if things kept looking up and she got the deal from Cal, she could stay in Yachats. She just really needed that deal.

She was ending the workday when the phone rang.

"Baughman Home Goods, can I help you?" she said happily.

"This is Wade over at Bucky Burger, and we're looking for some bark for the front of the restaurant. What's your price on the thick-cut red timber or the dark ash?"

"Ah . . ." Laura scrambled to look through the papers she'd organized last week, but she'd never seen a price sheet.

She ran out to the warehouse and looked for the clipboard Jake had shown her, but all she saw were dates and times of deliveries. Still no price sheet.

She put her hand over the speaker of the phone and called out.

"Mannie? Hello? Anyone here? I have a question from a customer."

No one responded. Wade on the line did, though. "Hello? Miss? Are you there?"

"Yes," Laura said, hustling around the warehouse, looking for any sign of a price sheet.

"Do you have a quote?" he asked.

"I don't at this time . . . ," she said, still trying to procure any kind of clue as to what bark dust went for these days.

"Well, we need it by next week. Do you have an opening?"

She ran back to the scheduling clipboard and saw some free time next week. An hour here, another hour there. Wait . . . how long did bark dust take to drop off? Probably depended on how much he needed.

"Um, we may have something open, but can you tell me how much you need?"

"Three cubic yards should do it."

Great, now Laura felt really stupid, because she'd asked a question and had no idea how to quantify it. What the hell was a cubic yard and how long would that take?

"Miss?" the guy said again.

Laura didn't know what to do or what to say. She didn't even know what it took to order such things or if they were stocked or how many crewmen this would take.

"Can I have someone call you back?" she asked.

The man huffed, clearly irritated. "Will they call me back with answers?" he asked.

"Yes," she assured him.

"Isn't this Walt and Jacob's place?" he asked.

She wanted to say no. Then yes. Then she realized that the reputation of Baughman Home Goods hinged not only on her father, but on Jake as well. And she was screwing it up.

"I can have Jacob call you himself first thing tomorrow," she said.

"You do that. Or I'll just go to Home Depot in Lincoln City."

The line disconnected, and Laura once again felt like she was losing control of something she had no idea about in the first place. And it wasn't just the business suffering, it was Jacob, her father, and possibly the crew if she kept trying to fit herself in where she clearly didn't belong. The truth was clear. She was struggling. *Trying* wasn't good enough anymore, and honestly, maybe she wasn't trying that hard with the warehouse. She was with the flowers. But maybe Jake was right. What if she was running this place slowly into the ground? What would her father say? He'd be brokenhearted if anything happened to the company, and Jake would be, too. She knew that to be true.

Maybe California was really where she belonged.

She needed to have an honest conversation with Jacob. It didn't matter if her pride or her future was at stake. She had to do what was best. What her mother would have wanted. Maybe she was clinging to something she should be letting go of.

After cleaning up and heading home, Laura didn't go to her camper; instead she went straight to Jacob's door and knocked.

"Hey," he said, opening the door. "Come on in."

She did and kept her head down. Until she noticed a pop of color that caught her eye. The centerpiece she'd brought him last week was proudly displayed on his kitchen table. And it looked to be holding up well.

"Everything all right?" he asked her.

She faced him and looked him in the eye. She wanted to be a businesswoman? She had to do what was best and have hard conversations. But when she focused on his face, she realized that there was something plaguing him, too.

"Are you all right?" she asked back.

"Yeah," he said a little too quickly and ran a hand through his hair. Crap, this was getting weird between them. Maybe he was rethinking this whole situation. They were sleeping together, after all, and then working together, kind of. Maybe he needed space?

Why did that idea make her lungs hurt?

She couldn't be thinking of emotions now. She had to think of the business.

"Clearly things aren't all right for either of us," she said. "So I'm going to start talking and you're going to jump in here in a second and we're going to be honest, okay?"

Jake nodded. "You're right. Honesty is best." He took a deep breath. "Laura . . . there's a lumber contract."

"There's also a bark dust one," she said. "At least, there could be, if I didn't mess it up."

Jake frowned. "What are you talking about?"

"A guy named Wade called from Bronco Burger. He wants you to call him by tomorrow morning for bark. Cubic yards of it. I didn't know what to say."

"You mean Bucky Burger?" he asked.

"Yes," she said. Great, she didn't even have the name right. "I tried to find a price sheet, and then I looked at the schedule you showed me, but I have no idea how long a cubic yard takes to load or unload, and so I had no context and just sounded like an idiot."

"I'm sure that's not true. And I'll call him tomorrow and straighten it out."

"That's the thing, Jacob. You always coming in to straighten things out is bad business. You said so yourself."

He glanced down, but Laura knew the truth without him having to agree with her.

Again, she reminded herself to keep her feelings aside and have a business discussion.

"Oh! And as I was leaving, I heard a voice mail come through. Something about Green Gables?"

"That's a golf course," Jake said. "It's one of our major clients. They don't order often, but when they do, it can be big. Do you know what the message said?"

She shook her head. She'd been too scared to pick up the phone again, and so she'd just run out the door and let the machine handle it.

Some owner she was turning out to be.

"I'll take care of all of this in the morning," Jake said. "Thank you for letting me know."

Jake's calm voice only made her feel more like a loser. She was messing up and he was being understanding? She was on the brink of losing it, because she didn't know what she was doing. And she had to be honest with Jake.

"Look," she said. "I'm worried I'm hurting the company. Maybe . . . maybe you're right and we need to figure out how to make this work, because I don't want to lose business."

"You did a great job with the shipment last week."

"It's more than that. You know how to run things smoothly. People trust you."

"They'll trust you, too; just give it time."

"We don't have time, and you know it. I just . . ." She glanced at the flowers on the table again. "I don't want to give this up. But maybe it's what's best."

Jake shook his head and looked like he was in physical pain. "Just hold out. You haven't heard from Cal yet."

"He's not going to hire me. I'm not as qualified, and Hannah told me Lincoln City's prices are better."

"You don't know that. You're good at this, Laura." He was silent for a long moment, and it looked like he was waging a battle with himself. Finally, he said, "Just wait to hear from Cal."

"If I don't get that contract, the flower shop can't sustain itself. The month will be in the red. You're right. The warehouse and shop are separate."

Something in her chest felt like it was breaking. But why? She was trying, but failing. And she felt like a loser. She would have to take the job in California and leave.

"You're Walt's and your mother's daughter," Jacob said, stepping closer until she could feel the heat radiating from his skin. His mere presence was warm and comforting. "You're a real Baughman. No one can take that from you."

The truth hit her just then.

"I thought this whole thing would make me feel closer to her. Help me find my place, my home."

"Your mom would have wanted you to be happy. If you're happy running the flower shop and not the warehouse, there's nothing wrong with that."

"It's a mess. And the flower shop can't support itself. I can't take from the warehouse without jeopardizing the profit."

And the truth was there in front of her. Jacob would do a better job running the warehouse than she would. And he'd worked hard for that.

But Jake didn't look overly elated about it, either. It was like on some silent level they were both grieving loss. The loss of her dream. The loss of what the business once was. The loss of the past. Because moving into this new endeavor into the future was scary and . . .

Lonely.

Somewhere along the way, she'd come to count on Jake. Even when she was a pain, unsure, frustrated, she was never alone in this. From the day she'd gotten there, he'd been, quite literally, within screaming distance. And he made her feel like she wasn't alone. He understood. Probably understood Walt far better than she ever could.

"I hate the look on your face," he said softly.

"What look?"

"Like you're hurting."

She was. So much. And she should tell herself to woman up and be a strong businesswoman. But just then, all she felt was loss. Loss and loneliness.

"Can you make it go away?" she asked him.

He stood close and cupped her face in both hands. "I'll try my damnedest," he said and kissed her. Soft but consuming, and she lost herself in him. Needing him.

Jake didn't know exactly what he felt, but he was pretty sure whatever it was, Laura was feeling it with him. Uncertainty, guilt, loss. He just wanted everything to work. And somehow he felt like the walls were closing in and the only safety net he had was her.

She kissed him like she understood. Like there was no one else she'd rather be with. At least, that's what Jake told himself. Because maybe if she really knew what he was capable of, she wouldn't want to be with him.

He cupped her face and deepened the kiss. Not fast, but direct. He couldn't tell her what an asshole he really was. That he'd made the deal with Cal. All he could do was wait. Wait and love her in the meantime.

But the thought of her leaving and the thought of her hating him were too much to bear.

She wrapped her arms around him and stood up on her toes as if to get closer to him. So he picked her up and she instantly wrapped her legs around his waist. He walked them to the couch and sat down, her sweet little body still clinging to him.

With her in his lap, he leaned back to break the kiss and look at her face.

"Tell me about your mom?" he asked. There was so much behind her eyes. So much she'd almost said a few times, and Jake had to know what had her wheels spinning like they had been.

"I don't know what to say."

"Say what you love. What you miss. Anything. You want me to make the pain go away, baby?" he asked and trailed his finger along her lower lip. She nodded. "Then I need to know what bothers you."

She took a deep breath, and with the tip of her nose brushing against his, she kept her eyes on his chest and drew a little circle over his heart.

"I loved my mother, but I'm worried I was doomed to fail her. That I'm doomed to always make the wrong decision. I chased the wrong choice, always, and I can't take it back. I tried to forget her and this place because I didn't want happy memories. They hurt. And now it's all I want, and I'm messing everything up."

Jake wanted to tell her otherwise. To tell her that of course her mother loved her and would be proud. That her father was crazy about her and was proud, too. But he let her continue.

"After my mom died, I wasn't the same. Neither was my dad. We were both like a shell. And for a little while, he treated me like the sight of me upset him. Reminded him that she was gone." She shrugged. "I tried to do everything right, but as the days passed, he got more distant. Like he couldn't stand the sight of me."

Jake closed his eyes and ran his fingers through her hair and touched her forehead with his. On more than one occasion, Walt had mentioned how much Laura looked like her mother. *Worse yet, she acts just like her, too. Always looking for something beyond this place,* he'd say.

"He loves you," Jake said. "I just don't think he knew how to tell you that back then. Or knew how to treat you. He couldn't separate you from your mother. That's on him, not on you."

It was the first time Walt wasn't the perfect hero in his mind. He was a man. One who made mistakes. One who was mortal. Jake loved and respected him, but Laura was amazing on her own.

"I just want to make them both proud," Laura said. "I'm glad my dad is happy. He let go and seems to be doing well. I just feel like I'll never find my footing."

Jake frowned. He didn't want to push too hard, but he continued. "You could have come back before now."

She nodded. "I could have. But I was stuck trying to be someone I'm not. Someone else. Someone trying to forget rather than live. I felt like nothing. I had to ask for everything, because nothing was mine."

Jake's eyes went wide and he made her look him in the face. "Your ex hurt you?" Jake knew she was divorced, but she never mentioned it and he'd never pushed.

She shook her head. "No. I hurt myself. I chose the wrong man. The wrong path."

Oh God, Jake wanted to hug her close and never let go. She was blaming herself, a habit she seemed to have had for a while.

Before he could ask more, she leaned in and gently kissed his lips. "Please," she breathed against his mouth. "I don't want to talk about this anymore. Please just love me instead."

Her soft plea made Jake's instincts kick in. He would do whatever she wanted. Whatever she needed. There was so much going through his head that he didn't know how to begin to deal with, but he'd figure it out later. For now, Laura needed him. And he would make this better. Somehow.

He kissed along her throat as her hands worked his shirt off and started exploring his bare chest. Damn, he loved her hands on him. Somehow, they managed to take each other's clothes off without having to take their mouths away.

Once they were both naked, Jake grabbed a condom from his discarded jeans and put it on. Laura straddled him once more, and the feel of her skin around his was a heady drug. She was all warmth and sweetness. Soft and delicate.

"Jacob," she whispered as she slowly sank down on him, impaling herself on his cock.

He gritted his teeth at the tight heat instantly surrounding him and hugged her closer. She moved slowly, up and down, circling her hips in his lap as she tested out every inch of him.

"You feel so good," she said, her hair falling around their faces like a curtain. "How can you feel this good every time?"

He ran his hands up her smooth back and gave a little flex of his hips. She gasped and ground against him, meeting his every move.

"I don't know, baby," he said. "Because you've felt way too right from moment one."

She kept herself deep on him, which he wasn't complaining about. She stirred on him; he could feel her clit rubbing against his pelvis as she did. She was getting hotter and higher real quick. He sensed it in her skin, in her movements.

Her eyes were glossy as she looked at him. She was drenched, only getting wetter with her orgasm right on the brink. He knew, because he recognized now how her little pussy squeezed him when she was close.

He flexed his hips over and over. Taking that last inch into her and watching her lips part on a silent inhale. He held her tight as she fell over the edge and pleasure wrapped her up. Pleasure he gave her. Pleasure he caught her in.

Tremors shot from his stomach to his cock, and he clung to her as his own release flooded his entire body . . . and heart. Because he was certain between the pleasure, pain, love, and loss, it wasn't beating right anymore.

But when Laura's arms wrapped around him and pulled him close, hugging him like she'd never held anyone like this before, he didn't care about his damn heart.

Because the woman currently wrapped around him already had it in her hands.

Chapter Thirteen

Jake heard a ringing that made one eye peel open. Phone. Not his. Laura's.

He popped open his other eye to see her scrambling from his bed and reaching for her cell phone.

"Hello, yes, this is she," she said, pacing in nothing but his bed-sheet. Damn, she was gorgeous, her blonde hair haloing around her while her bare feet hit the hardwood floor. "Yes? Oh my gosh, that's great! Thank you, Cal!"

Jake knew the news she'd just gotten, but Laura hung up the phone and jumped into bed, hugging him.

"I got the job for Cal!"

She hugged and kissed him, and everything was in motion for her to stay and be happy.

Jake should have felt relieved; instead, he felt sick. As if he had a permanent headache that wouldn't go away. This should be a good thing, especially after last night, when Laura had opened up to him and finally everything made sense.

And now, the solution of getting her the deal should be welcome . . .

But Jake's head just kept pounding.

She wanted something that was hers. Had been trying so hard for that one piece of her mother and to find herself apart from her ex.

"I'm so happy for you, baby," he said and kissed her. "I, ah, I have to go into the warehouse today to take care of a few things." Things like adjusting the schedule, figuring out how to make everything cohesive, and likely having to drop some contracts to make Cal's job work.

Laura frowned. "You okay?"

"Yeah," he said and kissed her. "The business is going to be great. The shop and the warehouse included."

She smiled. "We should go to dinner and celebrate," she said.

"Why, Miss Baughman, are you asking me on a date?"

She kissed him. Soft and sweet, and Jake's heart was in trouble. "Yes," she said. "I am."

"Then I'd be a fool to pass it up."

"Tomorrow night?" she asked.

Jake nodded. "Tomorrow night it is."

"Are you going to stare at your muffin or eat it?" Erica asked, sitting on the opposite side of Jake's kitchen table. The twins were playing Wii in the living room, giving Jake no excuse not to sit there while his sister hammered him with a scrutinizing glare.

"I'm just feeling off," he said. He'd spent all the previous day at the warehouse and realized he had to hire his replacement or lose three contracts, because Mannie couldn't handle the load all by himself and Laura had the flowers and design project to think about. Now he was home, and he should be happy that Laura was staying for good. He just wanted the business to be okay. To make Walt happy.

"Love is never easy," Erica said and took a bite of her own blueberry muffin.

Yeah, he could agree. He did love Walt and the business.

"It's hard when the business you're trying to do right by is in his name, though."

"I'm talking about the other Baughman, idiot," Erica said.

Jake frowned. "Laura? No, I don't love her." Sure, he cared about her. Liked her. A lot. But love?

"You sure? Because you're acting like you do."

"How would you know?" Jake asked.

"For starters, you're keeping dead flowers on your kitchen table."

"She worked hard on that centerpiece, and it's not dead."

"It's fermenting."

Jake shook his head. Whatever, he didn't care. He liked it. Dead or not.

"And," Erica went on, "worrying about her feelings over your own. Trying to keep her close. Feeling guilty because you lied to her."

"I didn't lie," he protested.

"You sure as hell haven't been a hundred percent honest."

"I'm trying to do right by Walt. By the business. By her. By everyone," Jake told her. And he had no idea how he was holding it together when he felt like such a failure.

"You're more worried about a man who is retiring and a place made of sticks and stones than the living, breathing woman standing in front of you," Erica said.

"I can't make everyone happy," Jake mumbled. The solution he'd come up with for Laura getting the deal she wanted and that the shop needed so badly was the best he could do.

"It's not about making everyone happy. It's about doing what you know is right and facing the consequences of that. You have to risk what you love to gain anything in this life."

Jake looked up and met his sister's eyes. Holy shit . . . he did love Laura. Somehow he'd come to care about her feelings over everything else, and that's why he was sick about all this. He'd risked the business, the steady income, the secure and slow progress. All so she could thrive and have her shot. And he had to tell her the truth. All of it.

≈

"I hear the floral shop is really taking off," Hannah said, wiping down the bar and getting Laura a mimosa.

She wouldn't call it "really taking off," but she assured Hannah, "I have a few customers and some regular business now, so it's looking promising. And I have that deal with Cal, so I can stay."

"That's terrific!" Hannah said. "So no California?"

Laura shook her head. "I haven't called to decline yet, but I will. Now that I have the Cal job, the shop will have its own money and be all right."

"Buzz around here has been all gossip about the future of Baughman Home Goods, and I'm just glad you and Jake worked it out. It must have been hard with the different deals Jake was trying to make."

"What do you mean?" Laura asked. "What deals?"

"You know, how Jake basically threw himself in to sweeten the landscape deal Cal offered you."

"Jake did what?"

"Cal was in here yesterday talking about how he got the entire Baughman team on his job. Said Jake saved the deal."

So Cal had only hired her because Jake had made him? Said he'd be there, too? She hadn't earned anything. Hadn't done this herself. Hadn't since day one. It was all Jake.

She was pretty sure a cubic yard of bark would have hurt less than that truth that just hit her. Jake had never had faith in her in the first place. He'd never wanted her to run the shop, much less the warehouse, and he'd had to bribe his friend to hire her.

Laura tried to swallow past the lump in her throat and remain casual.

"Yeah . . . it's been an interesting couple of weeks," she said.

Hannah nodded. "But hey, it all worked out. You both got a piece of what you wanted. You have the shop, Jake the warehouse, and everything will be great, right?"

Laura had to bite back a surge of pain racing through her chest. Apparently everyone knew more than she did about her own company, and the actions and deals of Jacob Lock.

"So, how long was Cal wanting Jake to work for him?"

Hannah shrugged. "Awhile. It was all he and Cal talked about when they came in here over a beer. Baughman Home Goods was supposed to supply the lumber for some log cabin subdivision thing Cal is building across town. And he wanted Jake on the team for a few months or something."

Laura thought of Jake's words from the past and realized one thing quickly. "Lumber for a subdivision sounds like a big, lucrative deal," she said. Something Jake wouldn't sacrifice his precious stability for.

"Yeah," Hannah agreed and dried out a martini glass with a towel.

Hannah didn't say anything else, but it was clear. It all made sense. Jake had made Cal hire her. Now she had a pity shop of flowers with no big revenue source she'd earned, and she knew the whole time Jake had been backing her up. She was never on her own. Never earned it. What was worse, Jake had known all of this the whole time, and he'd lied to her face.

"I've got to go make a phone call," Laura said. And she pulled out her cell and looked up the number for LA Marketing.

The fifth wheel in his driveway was shaking with movement. Laura was obviously inside moving around, so he went over and knocked.

She didn't answer.

So he knocked again.

Still nothing.

Finally he opened the door a tad and peeked in to find her turning the place upside down and throwing things into a suitcase.

"What are you doing?" he asked.

"Packing," she said, not turning around to face him.

"Why?"

"Because I'm leaving, Jake. I have a job offer in California and I'm taking it. I never belonged here. But of course, you already knew that." That time she spared him a glance, and both the hurt in her eyes and the snip of her words pierced his chest like a dull dagger.

"Laura—" he started.

"Don't!" She threw a shirt into her suitcase and faced him. "Don't you dare try to lie to me anymore."

She knew everything. How, he wasn't sure, but it was clear she did.

"I was trying to help. You can't just run away. Back out on a major deal. You told Cal you'd commit."

"And you *made* him hire me. So why should I stay? I never earned this. You can have it all, Jake. The stability, the money, all of it. My father doesn't need to choose between us. I'm gone. It's yours."

"So that's it. You're going to run. You won't be reasonable and talk about this."

"You were right, Jake."

"I'm sorry," Jake said. "I was trying to do what was best and realize that I was dishonest in how I went about it."

"It doesn't matter. You won," she said, zipping her suitcase up. "You wanted the business so bad, you've got it. And you have your lumber contract, too—all in all, it's a good day for you and Baughman Home Goods, it'd seem."

"Laura, don't do this. What about the flower shop?"

"What about it?" she asked. "You know as well as I do it'll go under in six months, tops. I don't have the clientele you do, after all. And everything I thought mattered doesn't."

"You matter," he said. "So much. You matter to me."

She looked him in the eye and hefted up her suitcase. "I don't believe you. And either way, you never believed in me anyway."

With that, she shoved past him and out the door and headed toward her car. She didn't look back. Didn't flip him off. Didn't do a thing. She just walked out.

Even after he called her name. Begged her to stay. To talk. She didn't.

She just got into her car and left.

It was official now: every woman Jake loved walked out on him. Only this time he couldn't blame her.

Chapter Fourteen

Laura had never felt a pain like this. Like her heart was being removed piece by piece from between her ribs. It was aching, throbbing, yet hollow at the same time.

She just needed to tell her dad good-bye. But he wasn't at the shop. So she went to the only other place she could think of to find him— Berta's Britches and Brassieres.

She walked in, the little bell ringing, and Roberta looked up from behind the counter.

"Hey there, honey," she said happily.

"Is my dad here, by any chance?"

Roberta shook her head. "No, you just missed him. He was going to the warehouse."

Great. There was no way Laura was going there since that was where Jake would likely be. And she needed to catch her plane if she was going to get to LA in time for her appointment.

"I'm heading out and wanted to say good-bye," Laura said.

Roberta frowned and walked around the counter and came toe to toe with her.

"You're leaving?"

Laura nodded and straightened her shoulders to be confident in her decision, but the way Roberta was looking at her, the way her eyes were glossy, made Laura's chest hurt. Like she was letting this woman down. A woman who wasn't her mother. And yet . . .

"I'm going to miss you," Laura said softly.

"Oh, honey, don't miss me. You don't have to go anywhere. Just stay here."

"I can't," Laura said, searching for some kind of solid ground, but everything beneath her shoes seemed to be spinning. "There's nothing for me here. I haven't earned anything. I need to get out of here. I have a life to get to," Laura said. A job and getting far away from Jacob Lock.

"Oh, honey," Roberta said again, and ran her thumb along Laura's cheekbone. It was such a motherly thing to do. "You don't have to earn love. You're wanted here. You're loved here. Just for being you."

A sting hit behind Laura's eyes. "I . . . I've made so many bad choices."

"You need to stop punishing yourself. I know things aren't perfect."

"I left my mother," Laura blurted out loud. The guilt was crushing too hard and she couldn't keep it in anymore. "She was dying, and I couldn't be around her. And when she did pass, I flat out left. But deep down, I was gone before she was. And then I spent ten years being treated like I was nothing and I deserved that—I just wanted to make it all right."

Roberta grabbed Laura and pulled her in tightly for a hug. "You hush with that right now," she said against Laura's hair. "It's hard watching a loved one struggle with illness. You weren't running from your mother. She knew you loved her. And I bet she didn't want you to see her like that, either. You have to let that grief go. And living ten years in misery isn't your penance. You don't need to pay for your sins, Laura. You need to allow your heart to heal and allow yourself to grow."

A tear escaped, and Laura hugged her back. Warmth, kindness, and understanding radiated from Roberta, and Laura had never been so thankful.

"I can't face him," Laura whispered. Because while so much of her past was crushing down on her, there was the matter of Jacob Lock she couldn't get past. "I can't face the man I love when all he sees in me is pity."

Roberta chuckled and held Laura back to look her in the eyes. "Honey, that warehouse boy of yours does not pity you, I can tell you that right now. He thinks the sun shines out of that slim behind of yours, and honestly, you should go easy on him. Men will try to give the woman they love the world. Sometimes they just go about it the wrong way."

Laura frowned. "Jake doesn't love me. He's annoyed with me half the time we talk."

"Well, sure he is—you're annoying." Roberta winked. "But you're kind and strong and so damn ambitious I just want to bottle you up and sell you on the streets." Roberta tapped her chin. "That sounds like I want to be your pimp, which was not my goal, but you get what I mean." She cupped Laura's cheek and smiled. "Allow yourself to be who you are. Because that's a woman you can be proud of. That same woman your mother would be proud of. The same woman I'm proud of."

Laura smiled. "Thank you, Roberta."

"Now, all you have to decide is what's best for you. Truly. If this fancy job in California is what'll make you happy, then go on. But think it through. For yourself. Not anyone else."

Honestly? She didn't know. Jacob had forced her to find her own strength, and she had. She'd run the shop and tried. She'd pushed through when there was no sign of hope. She'd clung to her mother's memory and tried.

"Laura." Roberta's voice was softer. "It's not going to get easier, but it's yours. You just have to take it. Do you really want to walk away from something you've worked hard to build?"

No, she didn't want to walk. To take on her life and make herself proud. Because she was a Baughman.

She glanced at her bag. "You're right."

"And you're a strong woman. Go claim your future."

With that, Laura hugged her and headed out to do just that.

Chapter Fifteen

"Well, I see you two didn't burn down the place," Walt said, walking into the warehouse, his blue Hawaiian shirt blowing in the breeze.

"No, sir," Jake confirmed. He'd only run off his boss's daughter. Jake had just shown up in hopes that Laura was at the shop, but he was greeted with a CLOSED sign and no sign of Laura anywhere.

"You know, running this place has been my dream. But sometimes you need to know when it's time to step away," Walt said. "You have the shop, son. All of it. You always did. But Laura . . ."

"I'd never take anything from her, sir. The shop is hers, but I don't know if she'll take it."

Walt smiled. "I see."

Jake felt like he was having a joke pulled on him. Maybe Walt didn't understand him?

"She's gone, leaving, and it's my fault."

"But the business is solid?" Walt asked.

"Ah, yeah."

"We're in the black. Slow and steady and responsible? Isn't that right, son?"

"Yes, sir."

Walt nodded. "But Laura's gone?"

Jake closed his eyes for a moment. "Yes."

"Was it worth it?" Walt asked. And Jake had to frown, because he wasn't sure he understood. So Walt clarified. "Was the responsible, risk-free choice worth Laura?"

That made Jake's lungs stall. He'd never thought of it like that, but that's what had happened. From the beginning he'd tried to be responsible, and that had kept Laura at a distance. Kept his true support from her. Then he'd tried to step in. All of this had been on his terms without him even realizing it. All for the sake of minimal risk.

"Oh God . . . ," Jake said and ran a hand through his hair. He'd messed up. Bad. And it wasn't just about the Cal deal. He should have tried harder to bend for Laura. Instead, he'd pushed her to break.

Walt just gave a short laugh and a loud sigh. "Oh, son, you have no idea . . ." He shook his head. "That girl is just like her mother. She'll make you work for everything—her attention, her time—and it'll drive you nuts. She'll always test the boundaries and risk it all, and more often than not, you'll lose your damn shorts in the process, but that's what makes life worth living. The color in a woman like that is an endless gift."

Jake glanced down and the sharp pain in his chest redoubled.

"I love her," Jake said. "Sir, I love your daughter."

"I know. I may be old, but I'm not stupid, son. And I can tell you right now that you are exactly what she needs and she is exactly what you need. But you hurt her again and I may have to rough you up a bit." He smacked Jake on the back.

Jake smiled at the only man he knew as a father. "Thank you, sir. Now I just have to find her and convince her that this is where she should be, not the city."

Walt laughed and walked off. "Good luck to you, son."

Chapter Sixteen

It had been almost a week since Laura left, and Jacob didn't know how to find her if he wanted to. He was seriously considering knocking down doors in California until he found her.

And no one was talking to him. An older woman named Cynthia was overseeing the flower shop in Laura's absence, but of course, the woman refused to tell him where Laura was. Roberta just laughed whenever he asked, and Hannah kept flipping him off every time he went into Goonies.

He'd officially started working with Cal, and Mannie was doing his best stepping up in his absence, which meant eighteen-hour days for him at the moment, because he refused to let the shop suffer, either.

However, Jake had no idea what to do with himself without Laura. His life was . . . colorless. But he'd taken steps to fix that. He just needed his woman back. He tried her cell phone several times and she never answered. Go figure. But she had to eventually, especially since the shop was here and she did care about it. Laura Baughman was the face of Baughman Home Goods, and he wouldn't do business without her.

She was a fighter and held on to little pieces of hope. She cared about the flowers because that's all her mother left her with. These facts kept his hopes high that she would come back. She had to.

Yeah, he needed her. Needed to fix this.

The rain was coming down hard, and he pulled into Baughman, determined to track her down. He needed to let his crew know he'd be in Wherever the Hell, California, until he returned with Miss Baughman.

As he parked, he saw a shadowy figure hovering by the front of the shop. It was hard to tell who it was with the sheets of rain coming down.

"Hello? Do you need some help?" Jake called out, running toward the shop door.

"Yes!" a snappy voice came back. "You want to explain to me why a lucrative floral shop is closed on a weekday?" she yelled. And Jake would have recognized that voice anywhere.

His heart jumped in his chest, and when he got under the overhang, he saw it was Laura, drenched to the bone and, from the look of it, attempting to break in.

"I was waiting for you," Jake said and went to wrap her in his arms.

"I'm not going anywhere, Jacob Lock!" she yelled over the rain and took a step back. "This is my shop, whether you or my father likes it or not. I'm building my life here, too. And this has nothing to do with loving you, because I also kind of hate you. So this floral shop is mine and you may have had a part in getting me that deal with Cal, but I'm keeping it on my own merit. And you can just deal with it."

He smiled and pulled her into his arms despite her protests. "So you love me?"

"I hate you more," she admitted.

"I never meant to hurt you," he said and held her tighter. He hadn't realized how terrified he had been that he might never see her again. "I swear, baby. I will never hurt you. I'll never keep anything from you again. And you have my support. All of it. I'm sorry."

He felt her sigh against him. "You were trying to do what was right by a lot of people. And you were trying to be responsible," she said, pulling away and looking him in the eyes. He nodded in agreement. "But don't you ever think to lie to me again."

"Never," he said. "I love you."

She frowned. "Oh no you don't! You don't get to be all sweet and throw that word around. I'm not going to be your camper bunny or whatever you think this is. I've been at a big flower expo for this subdivision project, so be prepared for me to turn this shop and your world upside down."

"I'm looking forward to it. And I do love you, you stubborn, sexy woman."

She smiled. "So long as you know that," she said.

"Now I need to show you something." He didn't give her a chance to protest. He just tugged her toward the truck and barreled down the road toward the house. By the time they got there, the rain had faded to a dull drizzle. He helped Laura out of the truck.

Jake hoped to God what he was about to show her wasn't too bold and wouldn't make him lose her again.

"Are you kidding me?" Laura asked as Jacob drove them up to his home. "Where's the camper? You came to show me I'm officially homeless now?"

"I just moved it. And I'll move it back, but first you need to see what I'm offering."

"You want more than half the business now?" she asked. How did she love this man and hate him? Oh, right, because he really was a good man, he just went about things backward sometimes. He also annoyed her to no end, and even now, she wanted to kiss him so badly it hurt.

"Oh, I want way more than half the business," he said, opening the door to his house and walking her inside. "I want all of you. If you're willing to give me a chance to earn you."

Her eyes shot wide when she saw his home. Things from the camper along with new items were placed all around the home. The walls looked like they were the same color as the living room in her childhood home. It looked . . . warm.

"I want you with me, Laura. All the time. I want my home to be your home. Our home." He knocked on the wall. "This paint was in the warehouse storage unit. Your dad said it was what he painted your old house with in the eighties."

Holy God, it really was the same paint from her childhood home.

Water lined her eyes as she looked around.

"I want to make you happy and give you everything. And you had a few happy customers step forward and speak for you that you were the woman to go to for such a contract."

"Are you saying that the flower shop has its own contracts?" she asked with so much joy she could barely stand it.

"If you want them," Jake said.

"But you made the deals . . ." Her heart sank a little because, once again, Jake was saving the day.

"No, baby, I didn't. It was your reputation that brought in business. In the time you've been here, you turned a profit and grew a loyal customer base that will vouch for you. I've been fielding calls for orders all week whenever Cynthia isn't around. You don't need Cal's deal to be in the black. You got there all on your own. That was all your doing. Not mine."

"I can't believe this," she whispered.

He took her hand and led her to the window overlooking the backyard.

"This is the last thing I wanted to show you," he said and pointed to a heap of dirt.

"Ah . . . you got me mud?" she asked.

He smiled. "It looks like that now, but here in the spring I'm told the best dahlias are set to bloom."

She stared at him in shock, and that water in her eyes threatened to spill over.

"What? How did you know?"

"Because of what you said. Because of things I'd heard Walt say in the past. He talked about Sundays with you and your mom. How you two would pick flowers from the backyard together. They were your mother's fondest memories, baby."

"They were?"

He nodded. "I went to your dad's old place and asked the new owners if I could dig a bit. They are in construction, so they didn't mind. Turns out, dahlia tubers—or roots, as it were—stay in the ground awhile. So I read way more than I'd ever need to know on the Internet on how to harvest them and brought them here."

"Jacob Lock," she said and threw herself into his arms and kissed him with everything she was. Because he hadn't just given her flowers or a home or a business—he'd helped her find what she'd been missing in all three. And he'd given her the greatest gift of his love.

"Thank you," she said.

He kissed her long and deep and finally pulled away. "There's nothing to thank me for. I can't keep up with all this." He waved his hand in the direction of the dahlia mud heap. "I need you to move in with me, marry me, and take over. Right after you go on a date with me."

She smiled. "So this was your plan the whole time, huh? Lure me with flowers, only to try to tie me down?"

"Yes, ma'am."

"Well, how can I say no to that?"

He kissed her again and picked her up, all but running to the bedroom.

Their bedroom.

In their house, where they could build a life together. And Laura had never felt more supported in her entire life.

Acknowledgments

Thank you, Maria, for being an amazing editor and incredible support system. Thank you, Jessica, and the entire Montlake team, for your endless amazingness. Thank you, Lauren, for your wonderful critique and edits. Thank you, Jill, for everything you do and the woman you are. You constantly go above and beyond.

About the Author

National and international bestselling author Joya Ryan is the author of more than a dozen adult and new-adult romance novels. Passionate about both cooking and dancing (despite not being too skilled at the latter), she loves traveling and seeking out new adventures. Visit her online at www.joyaryan.com.